"Bel is a lovely stylist, and her prose sparkles with surprising and memorable imagery: Discarded socks are 'tartan croissants'; cemetery steps are 'slug-snotted.' The dialogue crackles as well... The book threads the tricky needle of neither taking itself too seriously nor allowing its characters to become caricatures of young Parisians. This narrative is brief, but the feelings it contains are deep."   —*Kirkus Reviews*

"Bel fashions beautiful prose, punctuated, in the novel's fringed spaces, by her own poetry leaking love and despair in equal parts. The characters themselves are delicately fleshed out, their bond throbbing with undeniable chemistry, in a true testament to Bel's efforts—defined in the afterword—at writing a love story plagued more by internal conditioning than one beset by external obstacles."

—*Book Life* from *Publishers Weekly*

"A story that lingers long after the last page, not because it ties everything up neatly, but because it dares to sit in life's complications... Valérie's story is not one of easy answers but of hard-won self-knowledge, and it reminded me that the labels we wear are only parts of who we are. For readers who crave a novel rich with character, culture, and emotional depth, this book is a thoughtful and rewarding experience."

—*San Francisco Book Review*

ALSO BY ZOE MARIE BEL

Foothills: Poems and Two Love Stories

Stolen Neon: Poems and Two Love Stories

Zoe Marie Bel

VALÉRIE

OR,

RED VELVET NOTHING

SCATTERPUNK PRESS

FIRST EDITION, DECEMBER 2024

This is a work of fiction. Names, characters, places, organizations and incidents are either products of the author's imagination or used fictitiously. Any resemblance to actual events, places, organizations or persons, living or dead, is entirely coincidental.

ISBN 978-1-3999-9748-5

Designed and typeset by Scatterpunk Press

Cover photography by Zoe Marie Bel

'France and Algeria' map by Scatterpunk Press. 'Paris and environs' map by Scatterpunk Press, based on Eric Gaba's administrative map of Paris.

Visit **scatterpunk.com** to read more about all our books and merchandise, as well as to buy them.

*This book is for my mother Maggie,
whose meticulously handwritten French vocabulary notes
made France feel a little less foreign.*

Maman, je t'aime.

Contents

Maps

France and Algeria — ix

Paris and environs — x

Valérie (or, Red Velvet Nothing) — 3

Afterword on Adama Traoré — 123

Three poems, written in Paris — 127

Acknowledgements — 135

Author essay: 'Enough "misadventured piteous overthows" already! My intentions in *Valérie*' — 139

France and Algeria
NORMANDY
VAL-D'OISE
PARIS
FRANCE
TOULON
MEDITERRANEAN SEA
ALGIERS
ALGERIA

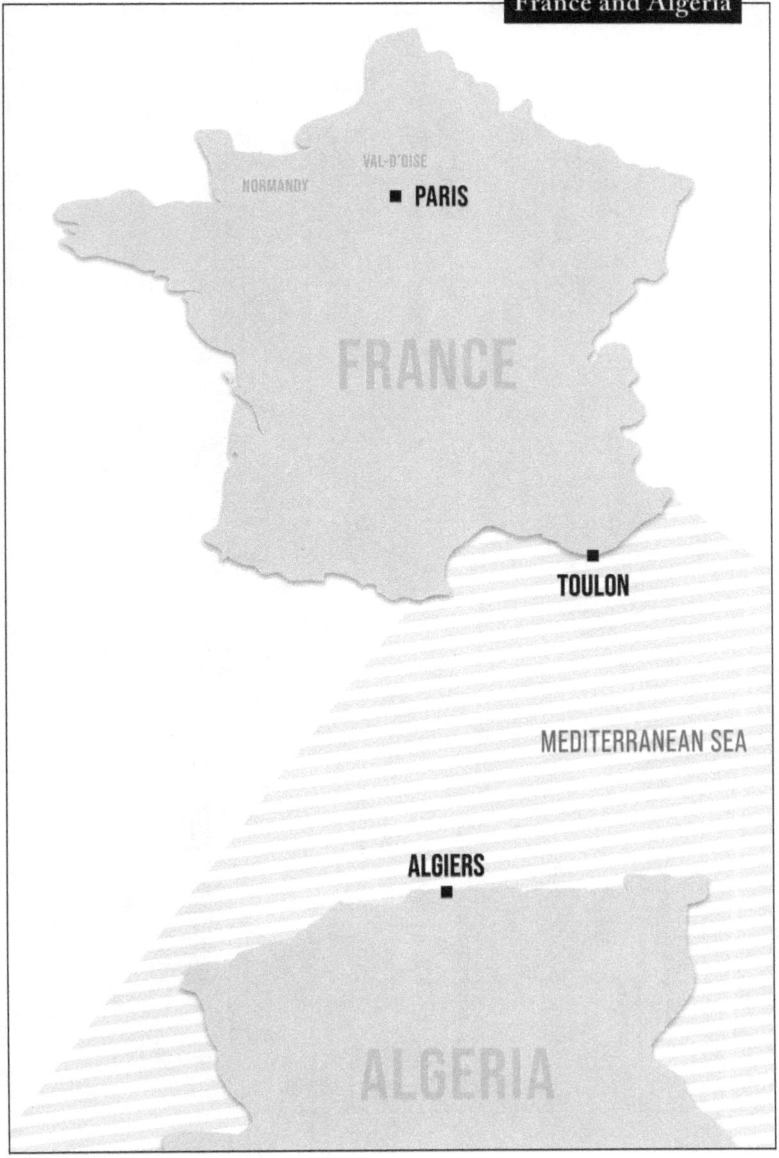

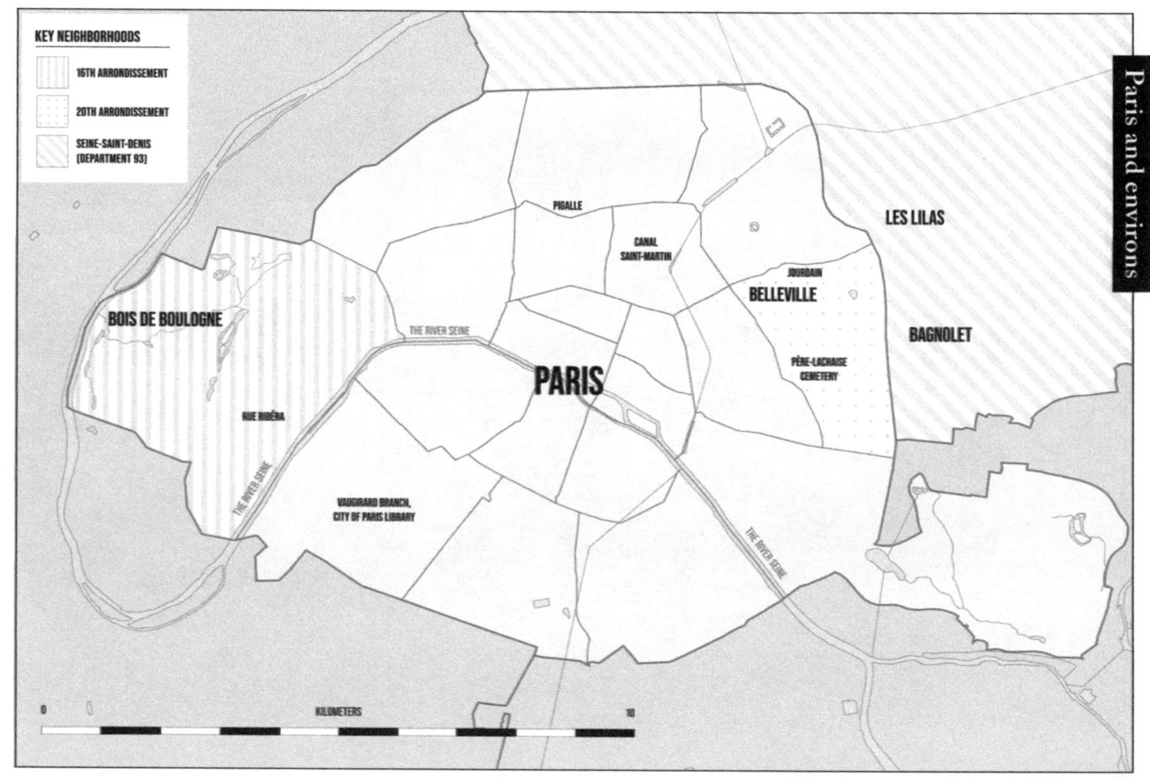
Paris and environs
KEY NEIGHBORHOODS
16TH ARRONDISSEMENT
20TH ARRONDISSEMENT
SEINE-SAINT-DENIS (DEPARTMENT 93)
PIGALLE
CANAL SAINT-MARTIN
LES LILAS
JOURDAIN
BELLEVILLE
BAGNOLET
PÈRE-LACHAISE CEMETERY
BOIS DE BOULOGNE
THE RIVER SEINE
PARIS
RUE RIBÉRA
THE RIVER SEINE
THE RIVER SEINE
VAUGIRARD BRANCH, CITY OF PARIS LIBRARY
0
KILOMETERS
10

VALÉRIE

OR,

RED VELVET NOTHING

The greatest love of my greatest love...

...is books.

Part One

JOURDAIN

1.

It was a Saturday afternoon when Valérie called, breathless. She was on the street, traffic honking in her background, and a pendulous crackling on the line told me she was running like hell. Nothing unusual there.

"Cél," she said. "I need you. I mean, if that's allowed?"

Wait. That was unusual.

She said, "Cél?"

"Yes." My mouth was dry suddenly. "Allowed."

"This has to get done, you understand? Tight deadline. And you've always been... you know? You're..."

I had no idea what words she wasn't saying. All the same, I said, "No problem. I'll do it."

"You're the best. The greatest! Thank you."

Her end of the line, a man started yelling. Raw-throated stuff about how it was a human right not to have to buy diapers for immigrants.

I frowned. "Are you *protesting*?"

"I'm late for work," Valérie said. "There's a protest in the fucken way."

"Ha. How's that taste of your own medicine going."

"No way, this isn't my people. This is Le Pen types. Someone put a hijab on that Napoleon statue outside city hall, and these folks just can't take a joke. One second. *Get out of the way, you creeps! What are you doing here? This is hustler streets!*" Val returned to the phone with, "Anyway, Cél, I better go. Catch you later."

"Val? Valérie? What is it you want me to do?"

"Oh. Oh yeah." Her tight deadline returned to her, at least for the thirty seconds or so before she forgot it again. "So here it is."

And so here I was, emerging from Jourdain metro station into the wind, heading for Valérie's apartment. With only a few days left of year 2018, redundant Christmas lights were swaying overhead. It was three p.m., everything looking a little grim and bleached out in that Parisian mid-winter way.

A kid in a Ronaldo jersey was kicking a soccer ball against the wall of the Saint-Jean-Baptiste church.

"The Lord be with you," I said.

He looked at me, head aslant, perhaps trying to guess what would happen if he spoke freely. He hadn't decided by the time I'd moved on.

Jourdain was a quiet, optimistic neighborhood above Belleville. There were still a few apartments here you could rent on a normal income, which meant a job that hadn't come into being with the internet. I couldn't say exactly how many address changes this was since Valérie and I had first met four years ago. Ten addresses at least.

With her fluctuating income, Valérie couldn't sign leases. She had "arrangements" with friends instead. Typically Val would pay no rent but she took care of the place, feeding the dog, or signing for packages, or vacating for a few hours when the owner came back with a rent boy. These were not always apartments, and not always legal. Sometimes they weren't even human spaces, insofar as it probably was not envisioned, when they were built, that a human would ever live in them.

But I couldn't comment on that. She was free, she said, living life on her own terms, and that was that.

Val's latest place here in Jourdain was an artist's loft in a former toy factory. Its ceiling was made entirely of glass that no one bothered to clean. On nights Val couldn't sleep because of the rain drumming on the glass, she would text me – an architect – for tips on how to shut glass the fuck up. I'd admit that her options weren't great. There'd be animated dots on screen for a while, indicating that Val was typing. Typing at length, the dots bobbing on and on. And then – nothing. No reply ever came.

(That happened a lot with Val. Sometimes I wanted them badly, all those written but unsent messages, scrappily amassed in a shoebox like ten years of receipts that meant nothing to anyone but me.)

As I rounded the corner into Val's street, I thought about how, as far as I could remember, this was the first time she'd ever asked for my help. It was a small thing to ask, really. I understood why she wouldn't take the day off work to do it herself. There was the lost pay to think about. More than that – and this was not spoken aloud, was something I had inferred myself – she *wanted* to show up at work. She'd finally found a job she liked.

When she'd explained on the phone earlier, Val said, "I need this done, and that's you, Cél. You get shit done."

It was nice to be depicted as some kind of no-questions-asked, all-hours-open body burier. It's just that it didn't feel particularly true. Or rather, it didn't feel particularly *proven*.

I suspected instead it was the institutional nature of this particular chore that made Val think of me. It was in the same universe as paperwork. Her other friends – gig workers, sex workers, weed dealers, cold callers, actors on a Transilien fare-evasion infomercial, songwriters arranging fruit in Franprix, serial students, serial interns – didn't exactly navigate that universe gracefully.

Arriving at Val's building and tapping in the door code, I got a doubtful nod from a guy leaning on the wall nearby. Early twenties, immaculately disheveled. I'd interrupted him mid-selfie, the red brick behind him apparently a crucial part of the composition. That's another thing about Jourdain: influencers. So many fucking influencers.

I headed to the elevator before remembering it required a passcard. Val's place was an illegal sublet: no passcard. The stairs, then. I was out of breath when I got to the top floor.

If I hadn't known it already, the yucca plant in the corridor outside would have told me which apartment was Val's. She'd been carrying this plant the day we met.

Using the key Val buried in its pot of soil, I let myself in.

The glass ceiling had originally been installed to help the factory keep its electric bill down. It still did that. Stepping into the light here was always like stepping into a bowl of piano music. I lingered by the doorway, let its fingertips work on me for a moment. After the rationed natural light of the rest of wintertime Paris, it was really something.

But I had to keep moving. Hard deadline, remember? Valérie's library books were overdue.

Twelve of them, in fact, spectacularly overdue and threatening to shit on her life. Today was Val's last chance to return the books to the library before they'd be classified as lost and Val would be billed for their original value. These were the massive tomes Val loved so much. They were about Egyptian hieroglyphs; the rise and fall of various auteurs in English theatre; the forensic investigation of famous airplane crashes; the design of Chateau d'If prison. This was *twelve* of the motherfuckers. The bill for them would be more than Val's monthly budget for food.

If she got billed, she'd have to "hit and run" the city library. This was her phrase for taking off without paying then never being seen near the place again. Over the years, landlords, lovers, friends and their mothers had all been hit and runned. Moving through the world now, Val had to hold in her mind an intricate map of where she ought not to show her face. Sometimes she forgot, remembering only at the last minute with, "Wow… yikes… no," and veering us down a Pigalle alleyway featuring a man relieving himself and a few broken swivel chairs. Change of plan, she'd announce a bit wearily, and suggest another route/bar/party.

"I fucked up back there once," she might add, or give a heavy shrug that said as much.

I'd learned not to ask by now. It was a money thing, I knew, and that was no easy subject between us.

In her call, Val had said the twelve books were "on the table below the Klimt painting". The Klimt would have come with the apartment, as there were only two pieces of decor that Val carried with her from one living "arrangement" to the next. The first was a photo frame that had been in her family for three generations. The second was the yucca plant in the corridor outside, which Val called a sculpture of her soul.

When I took Val's call, I'd been on my stationary bicycle, a *France Inter* debate show in my earbuds. (The topic: whether feminism had made flirting ruinous, or sexy, or – and here the panel seemed to coalesce – both.) Sundays, I might do a little work from home, get ahead of the coming week, but Saturdays were for unstructured play. I had a few coffee plans with friends – easily collapsible – and then a date with a certain fuck at seven, a fintech professional who dressed like an arms dealer and had no discernible emotional needs. So:

Yes, I told Val. I had time to go fetch the twelve books

and return them to the nearest library branch.

I'd been perky about it on the phone. In reality, there was an immediate nervous tang in my mouth. What might actually be dread, in fact.

Because here I was, alone in this space for the first time ever. No Val scissoring around in the corner of my eye, riffling and upturning and creating an epic mess in search of her latest improvised bottle opener.

I took in the apartment quickly, hoping the Klimt would be obvious and I wouldn't have to look too closely.

I couldn't remember who or what the owner of the place was this time. Very occasionally it was another artist. More often it was someone seeking to escape their own safe choices by orbiting artists. Straight men had a tendency to spritz the prospect of sex into the "arrangement", even if they were married, or 94 years old with only a knuckle between their legs, or fully aware that Val is a lesbian, generally with her hand in the butt-pocket of a rail-station pianist or a bartender with an Etsy sideline in scrap-metal jewelry. (Rarely the same pianist or bartender for very long, though.) Consequently, these days Val only considered "arrangements" offered by gay men and straight women.

This apartment read: straight woman, orbiter of artists. It had hardwood flooring, exposed pipes, and furniture with an Aztec vibe. The art on the walls was classical paintings recreated as pixel art. Val had to explain this to me on my first visit, because what they looked like to me was classical paintings recreated by an OCD child.

As I looked around for the Klimt, flecks of Valérie were everywhere. The tartan croissants of her socks, shed where she'd gotten bored of them. Her notepads, stacked near the bed – cheap, chem-smell notepads from Carrefour, discounted in a back-to-school promotion, meant for pony girls and rocket boys. Val wrote her poems in these, generally at right angles to the printed lines on the paper because it soothed her to reject prescription. There was mess in the kitchen area from the weird things she ate: peanut butter pasta; yogurt spooned into her mouth with a raw carrot; special-effects cereal meant for children (it crackles! it rainbows the milk! it's star-shaped until it's soggy, when it becomes a heart!). There were a few burst blisters of the ibuprofen she candied down throughout the day, every day. There was the bed.

The bed. Sheets left exactly how they'd fallen when she'd pushed them off herself this morning. The invisible ink of Valérie at her most honest on them. I thought of her fucking her latest girl there. That willowy blonde with the persnickety mouth she'd met at Supersonic, probably. Val spreading the blonde's thighs with her knees while her hands dipped and smoothed and found the unfinished sentences in the nerve endings and –

Enough.

I took a breath. A long, reprimanding breath.

Enough. The Klimt painting. The twelve books. Let's go.

Twelve books she took out all at once, and not in, say, humble lots of four, because that's Valérie. Twelve books, the overdue warnings for which had gone to an address two "arrangements" old, with Val only learning about them last night. That's when the "arrangement" owner had returned from touring his found-objects-drumkit show around the goth bars of France, and sifted through his mail. Twelve books that Val may involuntarily own soon, when she'd have to offer them to the Bercy homeless, because she couldn't carry them with her in her next move. The homeless would look at her like the fucking lunatic she actually is in that moment, and mention they'd prefer socks, cooked meat, phone cards, cigarettes or blowjobs. Val would urge the books on them even harder and say: these are your map to all of those things. And she'd mean it.

That, *that* is Valérie.

I saw the Klimt painting, thank God, before I could tap into the worst of myself any longer. I'd actually seen it already, without realizing that's what it was. Because it was "Klimt", not Klimt: a pixel-art pastiche of *The Kiss*. In this rendition, the lovers in bed were Super Mario and some blonde wearing a crown. I had a horrible feeling this thing had sold for a lot of money.

The books were stacked below the painting, just like Val had said. I kept my eyes off the bed as I headed over.

Then, a few strides in, something crunched under my shoe.

Glass. Broken glass. The size of a postage stamp.

There were multiple pieces of it, in fact, none much larger than the first, scattered wildly. My first thought: a panel of the glass ceiling had caved in. I looked up. Nope.

I followed the trail of glass. Very soon I saw it, on the floor by a chest of drawers. The photo frame.

Horror and sadness. For a long moment, that was all I knew.

The family photo frame Val carried with her everywhere. It was on the floor, smashed to pieces.

Val's father, Hamdan, was born in Algiers. Hamdan and his four brothers, plus their father Mustapha and mother Noor, shared a single room in the Casbah. It wasn't much of a place and you had to shake out the towels first, for spiders. But it was home.

When Hamdan was eight years old, French soldiers had raided their street at midnight, scouring for FLN bomb factories. The family had decided to flee, fearing the French army's broad definition of 'enemy'. Hamdan and his brothers were tasked with snatching up family mementoes, while their parents waterproofed their money and improvised safety measures for the climb down from their third-floor window.

They all survived that night, and forty-nine nights afterward. Then, on the fiftieth day, Mustapha – Hamdan's father and Valérie's grandfather – died of a heart attack in a fig grove in Béjaïa, one hundred miles east of the battle rouging the Algiers skyline. The joke enjoyed by the family until then was that, in their hasty evacuation, Hamdan had grabbed the wrong photo frame. The one he'd taken was of Mustapha's first fishing boat. The picture Mustapha would have preferred was of Noor, his first and only wife.

Nobody laughed louder at the mistake than Mustapha. All the same, Hamdan was pained by it. Years later, after moving to France and starting his own family, Hamdan had given the photo frame to Val, his youngest daughter, wanting to keep it in the family but not to see it every day.

That was the frame. The photo Val kept inside it, over the top of the fishing boat picture, was another story again.

There were only two people in Val's photo: Val and her mother Samia. In a way, Val's father Hamdan was present too, as a pink blur where his fingertip had crossed the lens at top right. Val was about sixteen here, all kohl eyes and go-to-hell mouth but still with a few questions in her face. She'd bitten into adult life early, but not yet truly tasted it.

The photo was taken in a parking lot in Toulon, often mistaken by the unobservant for Los Angeles because of its palm trees. Val would scowl that palm trees aren't native to California, princess. In fact, L.A. had imported palm trees to *copy* the French Riviera. (Of the many places Val had never seen, and felt no need to see, Los Angeles – and, by extension, America – was top of the list. Why would she go to a patchwork of imported ideas, when the originals were right here?)

In the hours before this photo was taken, Val, her mother

Samia and her father Hamdan had driven seventeen tins of home-baked *mkhabez* cake to Toulon for a cousin's wedding (in the sprawling Chaibi family of *pied-noirs*, refugees and street vendors, an enormous amount got accomplished through A Favor From A Cousin). The photo captured the moment after the wedding when the three of them realized they had lost their car, an unfamiliar rental because their own had recently been repossessed. Val and Samia, sharply defined in the metallic gleam of the Riviera winter sun, are gesturing to very different areas of the parking lot with the same fierce conviction.

It was not a flattering shot, both of them looking sweaty and uptight. You kind of wonder why Hamdan had taken it in the first place – perhaps to embarrass them into ending their squabble.

All the same, when Val had found this photo in one of her mother's rigidly organized albums, Val wanted it very badly. I think because the lineage between mother and daughter is so very obvious in it. Val spent so much of her time feeling at odds with Samia that a capture of the physical continuity between them was priceless.

Asking her mother for the photo would have been too much of an admission. So Val had stolen it, leaving a different photo in its place to disguise the theft and bracing for her mother to cry foul. But when Val next looked, the Toulon parking lot photo was back, reprinted. At that part of the story, Val's voice always fell to a wondering murmur. Reprinted.

Valérie's copy of the picture, inside Mustapha's frame. That's what went with Val from place to place in her complicated dance around destitution in Paris.

Or had done, until today. Now it was ruined.

I figured out what had happened easily enough. The frame had fallen to the floor from where it was normally propped on the chest of drawers. A wild glyph in the dust up there marked the frame's fatal slide to the edge.

Why it had fallen was harder to understand.

My first suspicion: cat. There is nothing dumber than a feline free-spirit. I didn't recall there being any pets on my previous visits, though, and a quick scan of the place showed no signs of one.

I considered the frame. It had come a long way a long time ago, and, made of inexpensive wood gesso, it had never been very strong in the first place. I picked it up just enough to scan for fault in the prop mechanism on the back. That's when I saw: there was no mechanism. Only a wire. This frame was meant to be hung.

I was sad for Val all over again. That's the thing about living in borrowed space. You can't put up picture hooks.

The leaning frame must have lost its feeble stance against gravity. As there was no way Val would leave the smashed frame on the floor like this, it must have happened since she'd left for work. Quite possibly *as* she'd left. For some reason I could never fathom, Val slammed doors behind her when exiting, but not arriving.

An architecture professor had once talked about the "moth effect". This was a play on the "butterfly effect", the idea spun out in the popular imagination from chaos theory. The idea goes that the flutter of a butterfly's wings sets into motion serial, miniscule shifts in the air that can ultimately bring down an airplane. In reality, this is bullshit, and pilots aren't rerouted around butterfly farms. In architecture, though, it's real. Miniscule structural weaknesses can indeed bring down an entire building, with enough time and repetitive strain.

I call it the moth effect, not butterfly, my professor said, because the outcome is always dark. People may die. People who trusted you.

As I held the broken frame in my hands… feelings. There were feelings.

I thought about the way Val carried this frame from place to place, wrapped in her favorite sweater. I loved her in that sweater. It was poinsettia red and − the single hint of its thrift-store origins − several sizes too large for her. She was constantly scooping up the excess that hung down over her hands and shoving it back toward her elbows.

She wore that sweater for the open mics in Montmartre where she'd render Rimbaud into street slang while a bare-chested guy thwacked a kettle drum. (Her own poems, Val said, were written to be seen, not heard. A few times I'd expressed an interest in reading them, and she'd looked at me with wary curiosity. Then she said: no, they weren't quite ready.)

She wore it at the pop-up art shows of friends, held in derelict parking lots, or former laundromats with fifteen electric sockets punched along each wall. She wore it in hospital snapshots with her sisters' newborn children. (Chaibi family tradition: congregate at the hospital, clog the corridors.) And she wore it for the vodka that every year she slugged from the bottle then spat into the Canal Saint-Martin, her ritual for her friend the "novelist" who had killed himself. (Val used the word *novelist* differently to how I did. Fabrice never actually finished – sometimes never even started – any of the novels he talked about.)

Yes, Valérie put on that red sweater for her biggest moments. And yet it was so inconsequential beside this photo frame that she used it as wrapping.

My hands felt clumsy around the frame suddenly, even this gentle hold on it too rough. I didn't want Val to see it like this. Wrecked, and so randomly, as though her most valuable thing meant fuck all to the universe.

And Valérie made to feel that way so often. The poetry no one with money seemed to want, even though so many of the shadow-economy dreamers she knew gathered for warmth around it. The doubt that surfaced more and more bluntly toward Valérie in the world beyond that circle of friends. I saw that doubt first-hand, whenever Val encountered old schoolfriends. ("Still the poetry... always the poetry..." Val would say flatly when asked what she was doing these days. Knowing by now that enthusiasm for her own story would only land as weird, given how static that story was.) Or those times in winter when we were forced indoors for coffee, entering the bistro together, shaking snow from our shoulders, and Val spoke to the greeter before I did. The greeter would look to me for confirmation, as though Valérie were a child.

What was immediately obvious to snooty greeters, and soon became obvious to old schoolfriends, was that Val didn't own a great deal. For young folks fresh out of school, this was to be expected. But Val was aging out of that grace period, and, in any case, had left school at eighteen. She'd had longer than most to build an adult life... and still hadn't. To own was to assert that you exist. What are you exactly if, at almost thirty, you own nothing?

That was the thinking. I knew it well.

Yes, Val should have a stable address by now, at the very least. And more than one decent sweater, more than one pair of shoes.

She should have furniture and kitchenware, and magazines that helped her obsess about both and buy more. She should have a savings account, a pension plan, an insurance plan. Because it's not enough to pay for life in the present tense, you must also fund the future and the conditional. She should have –

It went on and on and on. Ownership Pac-Man.

Val owned a potted plant and a photo frame. She ate

children's cereal and peanut butter pasta, and burrowed into the space of others who had the things she ought, until they needed it back or found a paying tenant.

All for her poetry. The poetry that no-one was buying. I had never outright asked her – it was one of our tacitly off-limit topics – but the impression I'd formed was this. As long as I'd known her, Valérie had not made a single euro from her poems.

I hated that I understood those who looked down on her. Equally, I hated staring into the black of the tunnel, waiting for a happy ending to crystallize. I could no longer imagine what that ending looked like. In the ten years since she'd left school, Val had probably fallen behind the version of herself that participated in full and sustained employment by hundreds of thousands of euros. Six figures. There were no six-figure deals for poets.

(Correction: *Multi-media poets*. I wasn't too sure what it meant – her poems, as far as I knew, were scrawl in a Carrefour notepad – but that's how Val always expressed it. She was a "multi-media poet".)

Val would never fill the deficit and catch up to what she could have been. She'd been poor so long that she was surely sealed in it.

Just a potted plant and a photo frame. And now that had become... just the potted plant.

I gently returned the frame to the floor and took in the apartment. Val had it pretty good right now, even with post-coital Super Mario on the wall. This place was the closest she'd ever come to *my* budget. But she could only stay here for a few more weeks. Then it was back to the spinning existential crisis of Paris on basically nothing.

I'd seen Val go from somewhere like this to sleeping on the floor of a trailer she'd broken into at a construction site. Generally, in that sketchier sort of "arrangement", she was not alone but one of a roaming group of artists with a similar conflict: too poor for a lease, too restless for social housing. Safety in numbers, she said – which, knowing her friends, including the dead ones, I doubted. But my biggest fear for Val was not that her choices were dangerous. It was that they were the only kind of choices she was ever going to have.

I thought it likely she would die prematurely. Not young, like some of her friends had done. Not Valérie, she was smarter than that. But she would die sooner than the padded assumptions of life in modern-day France. Condemned by all the marginal spaces and dubious imitations that had gotten her through. All the fumes from the warehouse perches, the gloop from the cheap meats, the coping mechanisms that nine out of ten doctors "did not recommend" because despair was something they only read about or cleaned up after. All of that would reach through the years and reveal there was a bill after all.

The moth effect in a human life. Tiny structural weaknesses, repeatedly strained.

It depressed the hell out of me. Sometimes, alone with my thoughts like this, I would get mad at Valérie, and wish she'd be more reasonable in her determination. (Was the ten hours a week she spared by avoiding a full-time job really worth living without a mailbox, a kitchen, a power source sometimes?) But I knew what Val would say. There is no such thing as *reasonable* determination. To be determined is to continue when reason would have you stop.

Staring at the frame again, I noticed something. The photo itself... well, what I'd thought was damage might just be debris and shadows from the jagged edge of the glass. Using my shirt cuff to protect my fingers, I eased out the loose shards and blew a few times to evacuate the glass particles and dust. Val and her mother met my eyes, their annoyance with each other registering now as annoyance with me: *What took you so long*. Because I was right. The photo was unblemished.

I looked more closely at the frame itself. It was wildly skewed for sure. But wood is a tough bastard. Think of the axe force it takes to bring it down in the first place. I would not be surprised if a professional framer looked at this "broken" frame and saw nothing of the sort. Some realignment, some tightening... that might be enough.

The glass, then. This was about the broken glass.

A few years ago, in one of my first jobs as a fully-fledged architect, I'd worked with vintage glass in a restoration project for a butterfly museum. If Val's family in Algiers had been wealthy, this frame might have used convex bubble glass, which would have been impossible to replace in just a few hours. This was not wealthy glass. It was entirely flat. Its only distinctive quality was a faint yellowish tint, and that was widely available now for those who liked a hokey "antique" look to their pictures.

A moment stretched as I thought about it. I couldn't replace an 85-year-old wooden frame from Algeria. But maybe I didn't have to. This might only be a case of some realignment, some tightening – and some glass.

I looked at my watch. It was three thirty. The library closed at six. The purest blood was hurtling through me now. Something I had felt only three or four times in my life before. A complete release from doubt. An immaculate alignment of the will and the means.

Valérie would *not* see the frame like this. She would never know what had almost happened to her most precious thing.

I put the frame into the bag I'd brought to carry the twelve books. I took a few pieces of the glass too, as a sample. That yellowish tint would need to be matched exactly. Val must never know it had been broken. More than that, she must never know it had been *fixed*. I didn't examine my aversion too closely, but I felt it there in my chest, hard and sharp: Val must never know I'd done this.

Soon I was turning away from the library books and recrossing that exquisite light back to the street.

In such small moments, whole worlds turn. Don't I know it. Don't I know it *now*, as I look back on all that happened next.

2.

It was my third or fourth apartment after graduating, a walk-up in the Saint-Germain neighborhood. Sorbonne students drifting around, gloatingly dowdy, thinking their familiarity with Foucault still meant something in this emoji age. My apartment was on the top floor. The view from its window smelled of pigeons but was precisely the skyline that other people dreamed of in Paris. My own dreams of Paris were more complicated. I mainly wanted it to be nothing like the rambling fairytale of Normandy, where I'd grown up. So far, Paris had obliged.

There was rain that day, so aggressive that I could hear its tattoo on the flower shop canopies from five floors up. My girlfriend at the time had more insecurities than your average newspaper in the wind, and for the thousandth time thought I was *emotionally cheating*. I was heading out to take her a box of the opera cake she liked and to screw her urgently against some ill-advised furniture, which always seemed to buy me a few weeks until the next time. On the stairs down from my apartment, I was vacillating from one step to the next over whether to go back up for a bigger umbrella.

Then I saw it. The yucca plant, advancing up the stairs.

A woman was carrying it, more or less blindly, dripping the rainstorm on the parquetry. She was young, about my age, but with none of my attempts to deny her youth. She arrived at the door to the second floor, and stood there jiggling the plant around, trying to free up a hand for the door.

"Here," I said blandly – no fan of gallantries – and opened the door for her.

She didn't seem charmed by the gesture either, and murmured, "Yep... thanks." Then she saw what was beyond the door and said, "Hey. Wait. Could you...?"

I saw her problem. There was another door ahead. Another after that one too, this being an old building in which fire safety had been imposed with the aggression of something seventy-five years late.

I assented blandly. I gave a soft snort of annoyance with the revelation of each new door, as that seemed expected. In fact, I didn't mind. She was quite something to look at from behind.

We arrived outside an apartment, one I would later understand was her latest "arrangement". Now she was putting down the plant, thanking me, introducing herself, and frisking her coat for the key to the apartment, all at once. She spoke hastily and with an edge of defiance, as though she'd hijacked the microphone and expected to be dragged off stage soon. I would come to learn that was her standard way of speaking.

She was Valérie. A multi-media poet who traveled light.

As she declared that and extended her hand for shaking, I got in full the playful eyes in which blue had annotated green. The sultana hair, braided with haphazard intricacy. The face I thought at first the work of Italy, but was in fact Algerian by blood, French in upbringing. French in name too, a stamp of her parents' immigrant determination.

"Céleste," I declared myself in return. "Door consultant."

This, she liked. As we shook hands, she said, "I guess you trained for a long time? The doors."

"I actually can't talk about it. These elite programs, you know..."

Yes, quite something from behind. But so much more than that frontal and smiling, as she was now.

"Well," she said. "Thanks..."

That afternoon the opera cake was wet, and the screw against the furniture particularly perfunctory. That girlfriend soon became another one, and Valérie and I have been friends ever since.

Parties, at first.

Warehouse raves in Clichy where the DJ (male or

female) wore nothing but a jockstrap and slaughtered the place with remixes of '90s cartoon themes: *Asterix*, *ThunderCats*, *Inspector Gadget*. Val first invited me a few weeks after we'd met, and repeated the invitation for months. Maybe she thought she'd get a quick read on who I was that way. A dancefloor tells no lies.

Every now and then, I would break from analytical cocktail pose and robot-dance ironically with whoever wanted to shake their tush at me. (I can absolutely dance, as it happens, just not to fucking *DuckTales*.) Valérie made endless shapes and conversation on the dancefloor, somehow both at once. She'd glance over at me regularly enough, giving a knowing smile and mimicking the robot dancing. Probably there was a hard and shiny aspect to the smile I gave back... hard and shiny in triumph. She was *watching*.

Next there were gigs for Inconvenient Wife, the punk band for whom Valérie wrote lyrics. The lead singer was a landscaper by day, so their drum-kit periodically got punctured by the rakes in her pickup truck. The lead guitarist called herself Juice, and wore a t-shirt that said *Black Queer Arsonist (Also Babysits)*. The drummer was a rotating cast of boyfriends or girlfriends, or – as a last resort – Valérie's coke-dealing cousin. The band were way better than such a formula had any right to be.

I'd watch from a sticky barstool and try to make sense of Val's lyrics. The lead singer's voice versus the instruments was like bird meets propeller, though, so I didn't get very far. Valérie, meanwhile, was bouncing around in the pit between the bar and the stage – a dancefloor officially, but barely larger than a parking space.

By this point Val wasn't watching me so much anymore, a shift having quietly occurred between us. She'd come up to my apartment one night, wanting me to listen to a passage by Gerty Dambury that was blowing her mind. It happened that my latest girlfriend was there. The girlfriend was a securities lawyer with her two-hundred-euro stilettos kicked off and her legs stretched out into the couch space I had just vacated to answer the door. There was a moment, but Val recovered quickly. She'd come back another time, she said, waving with broad cheer at the girlfriend as though from a parade float. I think the girlfriend looked askance as Val left, although the memory isn't sharp. None of my memories of that girlfriend are, in fact, as I soon got bored and ended it.

After then... yes, something shifted between Val and I. Not because it was a woman on the couch. I'm pretty sure Val had picked up on that already.

It was the kind of woman. I'd grown up poor – country-poor. Now what excited me was women with money. This was not at all the same shape of feeling as wanting men with money. I was very sure of this from observations of straight friends. I didn't want a provider; I made my own damn money. What hooked me about women with money was their triumph, and the qualities that had got them there. Men can shuffle into money; women generally have to fight for it.

Val had girlfriends too, of course. At one point, she and Juice, the lead guitarist of Inconvenient Wife, couldn't be in the same room without practically wearing each other. But over time, a consistency became apparent in the women we were each bringing home. The women I dated in no way ever resembled Valérie, and vice versa.

So Val watched me less. I still found myself watching her now and then, the way I think anyone would. There was appetite in Val's movements, and concision. A hint always of someone who'd known a lifetime of lunging and dodging and pelting for the last train out, who assumed this was her only chance in everything. You watched that.

Then, after a few months of my loyally attending their concerts, Inconvenient Wife disbanded. Juice had gotten arrested for participating in a banner attack on the National Assembly that put the words "Ministry Of Rape" on its frontal columns for a full three and a half minutes. Also, the lead singer didn't want to have to keep finding a dog sitter. The hunger, the band agreed, was gone. Which meant no more gigs in Pigalle basements rumored to have once hosted to-the-death boxing matches.

The warehouse parties became irregular too. I wanted music that sounded less like a microwave having sex. And I wasn't gelling with any of Val's friends. If there's anything more demoralizing than endless ironic robot-dancing, it's endless ironic robot-dancing on your own.

One night on the balcony of a house party, Val had exhaled cigarette smoke into the air between us, maybe so I couldn't see her face, and said, "How about just you and me."

By now we'd both moved out of the Saint-Germain apartment block where we'd met. Val was living in a friend's storage unit for a while, then a kebab truck, then… well, you get the picture. I had headed west.

I said, "That could work."

And so every few weeks we'd meet up, always sometime between midnight and sleep when pretenses were at their flimsiest. I'd come from Pilates, or an English class, or a date I didn't mention. Valérie came from some sort of chain-smoking artists meet where the infinite evil of Macron and rent were topics not so much debated as shaken up like cans of soda then cracked open.

In a group we were nothing special. But one on one… that was different. The steam of Turkish coffee tickled our chins as we sat at a sidewalk table so dark that the looping tip of Val's cigarette was the only report of her face.

She always got broody, those café nights. Looking inward when tired never made her happy.

"Trying to become the person I want to be," she'd say, "I've become a person I don't."

I never knew what this meant exactly. Was she thinking of all the people she'd hit and runned? Or her friend the novelist (kind of) who'd killed himself, whose pain had not registered with her as critical? Val had thought he was just experiencing the scraping days that came as standard with creativity. And she hadn't brought any more energy to the contemplation than that because of her own such scraping days.

Or maybe what was eating her was Samia, her mother. You never really get over disappointing your mother.

Samia and Val weren't estranged, not exactly. There were still calls about the babies of Val's sisters, about Tati deals, about the hints of Harman's alcoholism. But Val's sexuality, her resistance to full-time employment, her indifference to Arabic, her friends who smoked pungently, and loved catastrophically, and hash-tagged against the government but never voted, and rejected the words thousands of years had used for them in favor of self-descriptors that were at once vague and specific ("pansexual", "non-binary", "genderqueer"). None of these things had been among Samia's hopes for Valérie in raising her in France.

"She wanted me in the water," Val would say, "But not to get wet." To be in France, but not to be French. Or rather, only to be French in a certain way.

Val would tap off ash that tender way smokers do, then seem to put her eyes on me through the dark. I'd sense again the charged expectancy that came out in her, these nights. As though I had answers but was being cagey with them.

I'd propose that anybody doing anything even a little bit interesting gets their hands dirty. I was thinking of my own work as an architect, designing low-profile parking structures over the bones of blue-collar community halls.

In a leaning murmur on the metro train later, Val would

conclude: The important thing is to hold onto it hard, what she'd done, until she could put it right. Shame was her connection to her better self. She had to stay ashamed.

As Val murmured this, the improbable scent she had would come closer. Faintly volcanic cotton candy, that was her scent. Her watermelon lip balm probably, plus her Moroccan cigarettes, and then that soft hook, a hint of warm honey, that was entirely her own. I'd smell it in her doorway, or in the aftermath of her epic showers, or on the notes she left in my mailbox (tilting, knotted penmanship on the back of receipts that were clearly not hers: cat food, gasoline, hair dye, hundred-euro shellfish platters).

"Val," I'd murmur back, on the train, "You're so hard on yourself when you're with me. I think I know why."

A shrug from her invited more.

I said, "Because you know I'll never agree."

It was always then, on the metro train, that I felt the choreography of the mistake we might make, starting to work on our bodies. Val would be facing me fully but not looking at me, until suddenly she was. For a moment, the train would gently rock us closer as though in mockery of all the gentleness missing from the plans forming in my palms for her body.

Then one of us would break it – shift and look away, with or without an ambiguous smile.

Over time, the tally of that last-minute disengagement was more or less even between us. Sometimes her, sometimes me. It was with relief that I noted this. We understood each other. Understood that it would be incredible, briefly, and then disastrous, infinitely. Our feet planted in such different worlds. We were friends. Differences matter less there. That's where we should stay.

When Valérie's stop arrived, she stepped out with a meaningless, "*Adios*, doll," and didn't really look at me. The slam of the train door – nowhere more violent than on the Paris metro – sounding so very decisive. Such different worlds.

My reflection in the window the rest of the way home showed acceptance of that slowly returning.

Part Two

VAUGIRARD

1.

Almost a month had passed since the day of the twelve books.

Snow had poked its head into Paris then thought, *nah*. The courage of the New Year had passed, and the Bois de Boulogne park was no longer full of jiggling new beginnings in Under Armor, quoting marathon plans. They'd gone back to journaling instead.

I'd barely been home since January. Mail had piled up. The smoke alarm was blinking red for low battery, and the microwave still testified to the 17 seconds I had not used on something I could no longer remember.

Now back home for a while, I was fixing my morning coffee when Valérie buzzed. She was looking directly at the intercom camera for once. Normally she was half-turned toward the street and glancing back with incredulous impatience, as though all this fucking *administration* at my door was happening in the middle of a revolution.

I wasn't expecting her, but I buzzed her up before I could

really think about it. I did a quick scene check. There was fresh coffee. I was dressed a little messily, which Valérie much preferred. There was no trim brunette projecting her expensive education from behind an architect-branded chopping board. Friend or lover, a woman like that in my space always made Val nervous.

Very soon, she was in my doorway. Like always, she wasn't interested in coming inside. After that Saint-Germain apartment building where we'd met, I'd moved to the 16th arrondissement, and this neighborhood gave Val the creeps. She was quite sure that scraped on a cellar wall, somewhere below one of the hand-woven Ethiopian furniture stores, there were rematch plans for the French Revolution.

"Hullo," she said, the usual way. Not too enthusiastically and with a soon-to-be-lit cigarette bobbing between her lips. "You busy?"

"Not really," I said, the usual way too. Vague.

"Cool. So come on. It's a nice day for fuck all."

"Yeah. Okay."

Valérie was turning away when she added, "Bring your library card."

She shot me a look over her shoulder. A withering look, which I expected and deserved. Usually there would be amusement around its edges, though, the pre-forgiveness of affection. Not today. Today there was something preoccupied and unsmiling.

It messed with my breath a little as I grabbed my City of

Paris library card, then my coat, then a different coat because the first one declared my tax band a little too loudly, and so Val wouldn't be able to relax, and so I wouldn't either, when I really needed to relax right now. Because I could sense it right there in front of me: I could seriously fuck up today. Not *ha-ha-remember-that-time-when* fuck up. Permanent-damage fuck up.

I suppose that's why, since the day of the library books, I'd been... not avoiding Val exactly. More, conveniently busying myself. I trusted that, after a few weeks of no Val, I would know what to do.

In the event, I was sweating in my own hallway, unable even to pick out a coat.

We headed to the metro along Ribéra, a cobbled side street whose bone structure had little changed since Alexandre Dumas. Val had on mismatched gloves and I inferred from her one-handed flexing that the warmth they offered was mismatched too.

I said, "You're out of the toy place now?"

"Huh?" I reminded her about the place in Jourdain she'd lived in for three months, and she said, "Oh. Yeah. My next place is lined up next week."

"And in the meantime?"

She let a beat go somewhere. "Hmmm."

Off-limits. Okay. I didn't take it personally anymore.

I said, "How's work?"

"Oh." She shrugged and studied her cigarette. "I quit that."

"Quit?"

She looked askance at me. In my dismay, I had stopped walking.

I said, "I'm sorry, it's just... I thought you loved that job."

"It was alright."

"You loved it, Val."

"I love my real work. Poetry. Everything else is..."

"Yes?"

"Whatever."

I fell silent. Counting to ten, I guess you could call it.

The job – which she had most definitely loved – was giving walking tours at the Père Lachaise cemetery. To get (and then keep) the position, Val had to memorize grave maps, pronounce family names over stale madeleines with retired historians, and read up on the 572 ways to die represented within the cemetery grounds. The letter offering her the job had said they thought Val could help them connect with younger generations. They got that right. Children in particular loved the flowing coat Val wore as she led them through the graves, past angels with oxidized faces and up the slug-snotted steps to the southerly overlook, where loss felt a million miles away.

As we walked on along Ribéra, it occurred to me something may have happened that Val didn't want to talk about.

She'd crashed out of a job last year because her boss had offered her one hundred euros to let him eat her out in the backroom for PornHub. Before that, there was office cleaning, and the late-night worker who would touch himself as she emptied his trash can, seeking eye contact as he did so, daring her to make a scene. And generally, across all her lines of work, there were dick pics. So many dick pics. Most persistently from the former carjacker, now in his sixties, for whom Val had done courier work on her cousin's Vespa. Throughout her shift, he'd texted her addresses of clients with envelopes to collect. That was the idea, anyhow. In fact, five texts would be addresses, then the sixth text his sorry pile. Then the addresses would resume… and repeat.

When Val told me these stories, I'd urged her to report it to HR. She'd given me a tired smile, dragging some fondness into it but not much. This courier work, she said, was picking up thumb-drives with material on them for fake IDs and fake *Carte Vitales*. Or this cleaning work was in the backroom of a cash-only internet café that catered to the government-averse. "HR" was going to the rooftop to air an issue to your boss and only one of you coming back down.

Val must have sensed my thoughts as we walked this morning. She said, "Nothing happened."

"Okay. That's good."

"It's just… the job was getting too…"

"What? You seemed really happy there."

"Well, exactly. I don't want to be liking a job, Céleste. You either get that or you don't."

It was obvious which category I belonged in, so I turned away. *I'd* loved her in that job. It had articulated her charisma and intelligence. It was regular work with good pay. And there'd been HR, for fuck's sake.

I said, "You'd rather hate your job?"

Val shrugged. "I only want to be caring about one thing. Splitting my energies, giving the best of myself to two things? I might spend the whole day smiling but I look back and I see waste. I don't want to waste my life."

"Is this about Fabrice?"

The same open wound flashed in Val's eyes as was always brought out by that name. "Fab? No. He would have got it, though."

This was the dead friend who'd called himself a novelist. Val said this quite often: that Fabrice would have understood. Hearing this at times when I *didn't* understand, I'd be pissed off, even as I knew that was childish. Fabrice had killed himself. Understanding had not kept him here, with Val. And wasn't it the standing with someone that counts, even if that was standing in total confusion?

Val swiped cigarette smoke aside to signal she was done talking about this. She eyed me for a moment, clearly with another subject in mind, but it didn't seem much brighter than the first.

She said, "Where have you been these past few weeks?"

"Montpelier." Grateful for the easy question, I kept talking. "A conservatory refit for a lady with multiple sclerosis."

"Okay."

"There were other trips too. I've been working out of our

partner offices. Mostly eyesore-toning gigs." I saw that didn't mean a great deal to her, so I added an example. "A shopping mall in Lyon with bird death issues."

"Bird death issues."

"Too much glass. They fly into it." Shit. I didn't want *glass* coming up between us. I looked into the distance to get my face in order, and changed the subject. "So you're looking for another job? Something detestable?"

"Hmmm. I'm doing the courier work again, for now."

"Not dick pic guy, though, right?" A beat of dead air answered. My face dropped. "Seriously, Val?"

Val shrugged, and again swiped the topic away. She returned to puzzling over me with undisguised intensity.

"Alright," she said. "What the fuck is going on with you?"

"Huh? I told you. Birds, mainly."

"*Céleste.*" Val flung her cigarette away, then her eyes came back to mine and I was horrified: the something distracted and unsmiling in them was *hurt*. "You haven't ignored my messages, okay. But the person who wrote back was not you. This, here, is not you. Where are you?"

To continue to protest what she'd accurately sensed would be pathetic, so I fell silent. That's all I'd ever wanted actually: to keep quiet. To do a thing, but not have it *sound* anywhere.

Val snorted, "Tell me you're not hiding your head up your ass because you cost me a hundred and seventeen euros."

"No," I said weakly. "That's not it."

Actually, it was kind of it.

I'd just wanted to fix the photo frame, quickly and quietly. Disrupt nothing, leave no ripple.

Life, it turns out, did not share my vision.

D*assonville, Fabre et Hugo Architectes*, my employer, offered a service popular with its clients: framing the blueprints after construction was finished. So I'd had some numbers I could call.

I'd need a photo frame fixed express, I said. Two hours max. The can-do energy proclaimed down the phone in reply would have humbled Napoleon himself.

But when I arrived at the picture framer closest to Jourdain, the yellowish tint in the glass prompted an awkward, "... Ah." This particular type of glass was vintage, the framer said, and available only by special arrangement.

Same with the next two framers. It was five o'clock by the time I'd made it to the fourth framer – a vintage specialist in the Marais to whom the third had called ahead – and the repair work was done. (The rabbi who sat and watched his sons run the store had looked very determinedly open-minded when I confirmed that, yes, the fishing boat photo should also be enclosed in the frame, entirely obscured by the parking lot photo.)

Another hour went by in returning the frame to the chest of drawers, and sweeping up all the debris. I took a cab and hinted to the driver he could break laws and I'd look away, but it made no difference. I got to the library at quarter past six. Fifteen minutes after it had closed.

Twelve books. Thick, creamy books from niche publishers, some of them imported. Books that Val would now have to pay for.

In the immediate aftermath, I'd done a sort of hit and run of my own. I took the books back to her apartment and left a note: *So sorry. Call me, will explain.* (I considered pretending I'd never come at all, but I couldn't remember the order in which the books had been stacked and figured she'd notice.) On the train back home, I rehearsed my story.

I'd been held up by an emergency work call, I said, and hadn't arrived at Jourdain until 5.30. The rest of the story – the frantic cab ride, the locked doors of the library indifferent to my rattling – was all true.

"Emergency work call?" Val parroted, slowly and with an edge.

Sway issues in one of our marina builds, I said. Confidently said, because there *had* been a call about that. It's just that it had been the day before and above my pay-grade, so I'd been on the call to "absorb", not participate.

Val was pissed off, of course. But more than that – and I could hear it even through the really good impression of not giving a shit that she'd honed throughout her lifetime – she was gutted. I hadn't come through for her, after all.

If I'd let her know I was held up, she said, she could have called someone else.

I really thought I could do it, I told her. Quietly and with feeling, because, of course, that part was true.

A sigh, and a softening. *Jesus, Céleste... Okay. I'll deal with it. Bye.*

Lying to Val had horrified me. I'd wanted to call her back, tell her everything, so hideous was the possibility that she'd somehow find out I'd first been at her place three hours before. (As an illegal subletter, Valérie didn't talk to her neighbors, so it didn't matter that the influencer near the entrance had seen me. But I couldn't shake off the babbling paranoia that somewhere, somehow, there'd be a time-stamp of my true arrival that Val could access.)

But I had overruled my every shrill impulse, locked my phone inside my mailbox and gone out to drink too much and laugh too hard and seduce too generically. Because if I told Val everything, that would be far, far too close to *everything*. And what had expressed itself in me, as I'd held the broken photo frame that afternoon, was not meant for Val to know. It was mine. The paper plane that was perfect so long as it stayed in my hand.

Drifting along Ribéra now, with faltering piano scales from a high window above us, I said, "I told you I'd pay for the books."

"And I told you," Val said, "Your money hasn't suddenly

gotten takeable."

I knew that, of course, it was just something to say. Val paid her own way, or she went without. She might have masking tape on a shaving cut because she couldn't afford a Band-Aid. Tap water on her cereal because ditto milk. Shoes that suggested she'd participated in the construction of a continental railroad. All the same, she meant it – she didn't want your damn money.

Some of the women she dated didn't get it and lost her suddenly and completely after offering to pay the bill one too many times. They thought that was to love her, but Val felt it as to *edit* her. Buy me a chateau, she said, and I'd still camp out by just one window, drinking the light from it into my poems.

I knew that, and it's why my fuck-up with the books was so mortifying. I'd created a problem she wouldn't let me fix. I'd made her even poorer.

I said, "Of course I'm not going to pay. I was being polite."

"What are you – English? A serial killer? I don't want polite."

I knew that too.

"Here." I offered the library card she'd asked me to bring. "I'll have to come with you every time. But consider this yours."

"Codependency," Val said flatly. "Fantastic."

All the same, she took the library card. Too close to the metro to start another cigarette, she dug out an ibuprofen instead. Out on the street she kept them in her pocket like loose change.

I said, "Headache?"

Every now and then I didn't want to pretend I hadn't noticed her pill-popping. I always used this same singsong voice to float some excuse for her doing it.

Val looked wry, but then seemed to think about it. Actually, now that I'd mentioned it, "Yeah… I didn't sleep so great last night."

In silence I invited more detail of her present living arrangement. She avoided my look and said, "It's only for a few more days."

By daylight Val was generally moody because not generally awake. Only amid the smudged perimeters of night did she fully unfurl. All the same, there was no doubt about it now: today's moodiness was new. Damn to hell and back those twelve books.

As we arrived at the metro station and took the steps down, Val considered the library card. She said, "We'd better go to Vaugirard. No one knows me there. They won't get in my face."

I thought threat assessment of specific library branches was a bit unnecessary. But the library situation had somehow spiraled into a world I didn't engage with at all – social media – so what did I know.

"Sounds good," I said.

I felt the press of Valérie from behind as she walked with me through the ticket barrier, both of us on my fare tap. An alarm went off as sensors detected the fare evasion, and a few heads turned. I'd been embarrassed by this habit of Val's at first, until she'd pointed out there were no alarms like that for tax dodgers. Imagine, she said, if you couldn't pass through without the alarm sounding unless you'd paid what you rightfully owe on your income. No hiding it in a corporation in Ireland. The barriers of the 16th arrondissement would be howling like a bitch on heat.

I was still kind of embarrassed, but it was by the whole wretched system now.

On the train, we sat by a sweet, possibly homeless woman doing Sudoku. I could sense her antenna go up at the weighted silence between Val and I. The woman was right: it was a strange silence, ticklish with mutual awareness. But I didn't dislike it and Val didn't seem to either. In the glass of the opposite window I could see we were almost looking at each other.

Representatives of France's favorite pastime, apocalyptic protest, boarded the train at Boissière, heading for Nation with the absurd route-inefficiency of out-of-towners. There were a lot of Sharpied signs asserting '____ rights are human rights' but that first word was different every time, so it was hard to grasp exactly what their beef was. The Sudoko lady, clucking annoyance as the protestors surged onboard, scurried off to another seat. A protest kid in a Viking helmet with tampons dangling from its horns took her place, and Valérie's hand went into my coat pocket.

Slipped inside my pocket, for warmth, that was how I

was to understand it. I agreed and didn't look at her. Didn't do very much, in fact. Just let it vibrate in me softly, like the blended hum of our two minds. Something was up but, just for a minute, Val was bored with it.

Val said, "That's sad about the birds. Flying into the glass."

"The cruel thing is," I said, "They think it's more sky."

It occurred to me that, in the few seconds before they were brained on the window, the birds might experience this illusion of more sky not as cruelty but as joy. I kept quiet, though. I wasn't the kind of person who could pull off a thought like that. I'd sound like I was quoting someone, and not quite correctly.

Valérie was watching me carefully, perhaps sensing unexpressed thoughts.

"But that's happiness," she said. "No?"

And I rather wished I'd said it after all.

2.

W e got off the metro at Trocadéro, and took Vélib pedal bikes down to the Vaugirard branch of the city library. Whenever she returned a bike to the bike-share rack, Val liked to leave in the handlebar basket some anonymous words for the next rider. Vague words to which they would bring their own context. Val scrawled them across baguette paper or whatever other inscribable trash a previous rider had left there.

Today's words were: *I bet you didn't think you could do it.*

Val shrugged unenthusiastically, called it not her best.

Now that the library was right by us, we paused for a moment.

Val said, "Oh boy."

"Yep," I said.

Vaugirard was a small and involuntarily intimate library, but its shelves were eclectic and there were black leather couches where fine old dames would sit with Obama's memoir and pick their noses very discreetly (which in their minds meant very slowly). My lycée was only a few blocks away, so teenage memories dripped here and there, but I shrugged them off. At a certain age you realize that your stupid years don't exist anywhere, not with any meaningful accuracy – you are their only meticulous archive. I'd been a diabolical teenager, glib and treacherous at the center of undeserved adoration. But those who knew that would never congregate and bring it together. I could let it go.

No, if Val and I were standing by the library nervously, it was the more recent past that was to blame.

After I'd failed to return the books that Saturday, Val had done it herself on her next day off. She explained the situation: wrong addresses, useless friends. But the library had already generated the bill for replacing the twelve books and would not revoke it, even with the books back on its shelves. Valérie, they said, had had *many* chances. She also, it was presumed, had a conscience. Somewhere between those two things, Val should have made right the hole she was leaving in other people's learning, and sometime far sooner than now.

In the letter accompanying the bill for the books, Val was given a choice. Don't pay the bill and lose her library membership, with shadows forever attached to her name but no dogs sent out. Or: pay up and retain her membership. Lesson learned, and conscience hopefully and duly defibrillated.

But Val simply did not have the money, and would never have it. Not if she was to eat as well. So there was no real choice for her.

Val's library card was revoked. She could no longer take out the books that so many times had made her feel she wasn't poor. She had accepted it without a word, but her sadness, I knew, was enormous.

That would have been that, if Val's friend/ex Juice hadn't seen the letter from the library. Now that Inconvenient Wife had disbanded, Juice was a full-time "artivist" on Instagram. This meant she sprayed anti-Macron graffiti on revered buildings, then published photos and making-of videos under handle PussySpatter.

Juice took a photo of the letter and posted it to her 100k followers, with hashtags #finedout #parismafia. Val wasn't on social media because it was "basically shouting into a bucket", and asked Juice to black out her name in the letter before posting. (Val believed in libraries, for fuck's sake, and didn't want to be outed as a slutty borrower.) This turned out to be a very good move, because the letter went viral. A small but global kerfuffle on the internet ensued.

In response to the outcry, the City of Paris Library promised on Twitter to "review, reflect on and learn, true to the spirit of a library". Followers hoped this meant Valérie would receive a pardon in the mail (still two addresses wrong), but none had yet arrived and Val herself had no such expectation. A library in Berkeley freaking California might cave, she said, but not one in France. You could be poor here so long as you were slavish to the rules.

Despite the blacked out name, there was enough

situation-specific language in the letter for the library to figure out who'd leaked it to Instagram. The question was: could the library be bothered? *Institutionally* bothered, that is. One or two of them figuring it out would mean nothing, unless they followed up with phone calls to others who also gave a shit. Did librarians have that kind of time, that kind of animus?

During my time out of town, Val and I had discussed this question on text. We'd both admitted we didn't have a clue what librarians were capable of. Val remembered once reading about a librarian in Saint-Malo who'd hidden rolled-up pages of Verlaine in her cooch to save them from the invading Nazis. But it was hard to draw from that a general principle relevant to the present situation.

Outside the library door now, I said, "We calmly leave, okay? If they say anything."

Val nodded nervously. "I kind of wish Juice had lost her shit some other way over this whole thing."

"How? Arson?"

"No, she's sworn off that. All the smoke, you know. Not eco-friendly."

"Oh." I joined Val in smiling. It was good to feel laughter connect us for a moment again. Val seemed to feel it too, and put her hand a few inches from mine on the door handle.

"Comrade," she said.

"Let's do this," I nodded.

Just as we were about to pull on the doors, Val's other

hand darted out and stopped me.

New emotion suddenly surfaced in her eyes. It was unrecognizable to me, at least in the glance I got before she said, "Céleste –"

"Ladies. If you please."

A gentleman with birdwatching vibes was behind us, not thrilled by our obstruction of the entrance. Val sighed, opened the door, and gallantly motioned him inside.

Once we were alone again, I said, "Was there something…"

"No," Val said tentatively. Then firmly, "No. Let's get this over with."

We entered the library. No one at reception hit an alarm under the desk, or even gave us a second glance. Either the library outsourced their menace to midnight snatch teams, or no one gave a shit about social media.

Once we were beyond earshot of the librarians, I said as much to Val. I added, "You can still come in and read whenever you want."

Val agreed vaguely. Moody again. That weird moment at the door apparently still on her mind. What had she been about to say? I almost insisted she tell me.

But she drifted off down an aisle, and I didn't follow. In general she disliked anyone puppying along after her at the library – this was her discovery place. And it seemed she could particularly use a break from me right now.

So I took one of the black leather chairs and flipped through a few books that were lying around. Unless they were spectacular buildings, libraries didn't thrill me.

When Val came back a little later, I had my nose in an autobiography of Jazz-age model Kiki de Montparnasse. A policeman in Nice had just called Kiki a whore and she'd slapped him. That was how Kiki de Montparnasse's days seemed to go.

I looked up slowly and saw Val had no books in her hands and wasn't smiling.

"By the way..." She clicked something down onto the lamp table. "You missed a bit."

She turned on her heel and left me staring at it. A piece of glass. Broken glass. About the size of a postage stamp and with a yellowish tint.

A moment went somewhere.

Let me be clear. I'd checked the floor of her apartment. Painstakingly checked it. The hipster fucking hardwood must have sent this piece of glass somewhere out of sight.

I touched it. Lightly, I thought, although a pinhead of blood immediately formed and I watched without interest.

Then, without knowing what I was doing, only that I had to, I followed Val.

She hadn't gone far. She was at the dead-end of an aisle, staring too vaguely at the books on offer.

"Valérie..."

She didn't look up. "I always turn *pépé's* frame toward Algiers. I noticed straightaway it had been moved. And it was too shiny. Like someone had polished it. You ever seen a maid at my place?"

"I... no."

"Then I was looking around for a power socket, and I found that glass on the floor." Val left some silence. When I didn't break it, she said, "What the fuck, Céleste?"

"I wanted to just take care of it."

"That's why you didn't get to the library in time? You were fixing it?" At my nod, her eyes fell away. "So you lied."

"I hate that I did." I moved closer, jolted by an impulse to do more than talk.

"*Emergency work call.*" A harsh laugh broke out of Val's throat as she savored that. "Then you're a weirdo for weeks. 'Work'. 'Away with work'."

"I *was* away with work."

Confusion was Val's most hated emotion and became anger very quickly. I think because it tapped on her biggest fear: that, beneath it all, she didn't measure up.

She was angry now, and flung out her hand at nothing. "What is the matter with you? You broke it, okay. But then you fixed it. How could I be mad at you when you fixed it? There was no need to lie."

"No," I said, horrified. "No, I didn't break it. It was like that when I got there."

I watched Val's confusion fall apart... and then reform in a different way. "What? You found it there... and then you fixed it?"

"Exactly."

Exasperated now: "Then I'm asking again, even louder. Why the fuck did you lie?"

"I just wanted to..." I let that trail off and took a minute. "Carry on as we are."

Those words spoken aloud were so much larger than I'd expected. *Carry on as we are.* Did they sound that way to Valérie too?

I think so. Her face was shifting. It looked like I had, with those words, started to make sense. A sad kind of sense.

She turned away, fingertipped a book spine. "You wanted to be kind to me, and then deny it."

I said nothing, realizing that wasn't exactly untrue.

Val slumped back against the bookshelf and closed her eyes, took care of some things in them that she didn't want me to see. She had absented herself by closing her eyes like that, or I'd have reached to her. When she opened them again, the hurt I'd glimpsed earlier had returned, and her voice was scraped and small.

She said, "This isn't the first time, and you know it. Four texts: 'I'm coming'. Fifth text: 'I'm stuck at work' –"

"I *am* stuck at –"

"Please. You're an architect, not a paramedic. They urgently need you around for 'bird issues'? Just stop. Work is your excuse."

Our eyes met, all self-consciousness gone. I was getting angry myself now. At least, I thought it was anger. The rising thrum of something.

Val said, "You just won't be in the light with me. You shove me away with your silences, your work trips, your explanation gaps. It's like you don't want to make sense, you're terrified of it actually, and you don't care if I get ripped to shit in the meantime. You make me crazy." She swallowed and stood a little taller. "I have waited and *waited* for you to explain."

She made to elbow past me and I think we both assumed I'd step back. But then I found it was in me again, just as suddenly as it was there before, when I was holding the broken frame.

Elemental certainty. Conviction in my bones that was its own permission.

I took hold of Val's coat to stop her from leaving, and I went to her ear.

I said, "I think I love you with every cell in my body."

The thin light of the window above us felt harsh suddenly. I closed my eyes and gripped her, even made a hushing sound, as though if neither of us moved or breathed, it might just lumber past us, what I'd just said, and we'd be alright.

Then Val's hands rustled up through the pressing points of our bodies and found my face. She eased my cheek back from hers in an invitation to look. I looked. Her eyes were a tangle of happy and sad.

Softly she said, "Walk."

3.

We walked.

Paris, always so much itself, was suddenly anywhere. The slapping footfalls on the wet sidewalks, the infinite binaries of red, green, stop, go. It had nothing to do with us, we walked in softly vibrating isolation. My muscles felt sore and quivery, all because of words. The human nervous system, triggered by lunges in our own souls as much as by lunges from the shadows. How funny we are.

A drizzle had started, itty-bitty kisses on my skin. I looked over at Valérie, saw the rain speckling her hair. Only one glove on now... had she lost the other? Probably. The dropped mitten was her special talent. I thought of her whenever I saw loner mitts in all the nooks of the city where lost things slump. I wanted to rescue them, stuff them in a drawer, tell nosy houseguests they were for window cleaning. Then, when Val next showed up at my door fresh from a mitten dropping, I'd have my moment.

Of course, I never actually did it. My mind went just

about anywhere in my thoughts of Val, but only because in reality there was the safety of no movement.

And now here we were. Moving.

What came next, I couldn't imagine. There was no thinking beyond what I'd just done, which felt at once wildly new and deeply historical. What it didn't feel, and this surprised me, was wrong. The winter air tasted clean in my mouth, and the marvel of being here in this my body, with these my thoughts, was, for a moment, enormous.

With both of us seeming to be following the other, we found the Seine. Valérie sat down on the riverside edge, dangled her feet over the water. As I joined her –

"Wait," she said. "You hate this."

Meaning the cigarette she'd just brought out from her pocket.

I thought about denying it. Then I found myself smiling. "Why does that matter suddenly?"

Val didn't know. She didn't light up, though. She tucked the cigarette behind her ear and we watched the Seine complicate the color green. The rain had stopped, for now.

She motioned back toward the library. "Why'd you say it like that?"

"What do you mean?"

"Sad. Unbearable, even."

That surprised me. I'd thought this was something we both understood. I read her face for a moment and saw that I wasn't necessarily mistaken. Maybe she just wanted to compare intuitions.

I said, "It wouldn't work."

She was quiet. "No?"

"Look at us, Val. How different we are."

"*Who* looking at us? The world looking?"

"I don't..."

She pressed, "Are we so different when it's just you looking?"

"I don't know how to separate those things. Or if they can be separated."

Val snorted. "I've seen you dance, Cél. You don't give a shit what anyone else thinks."

"I can't imagine..." I trailed off. There were so many things I couldn't imagine. Introducing Val to my mother, for example. *Multi-media poet*, I'd say. My mother would coo and with a stretched smile say, *And where might I have seen your work?* And Val... Val would get out her latest scrap of notepaper.

"Fuck imagining," Val said. "If you can imagine it, it's already familiar. It's boring."

"Okay. But leaps in the dark are overrated. Ask an emergency room."

She laughed at that, despite herself. "But then you go out instead the way most people do. All the lights safely on, and too much food, booze and smokes." Before I could come back on that, "Céleste, you're still not really talking to me. All the things you've said so far are also reasons for us not to be *friends*. They didn't stop you all these years."

I let the truth of that sit for a minute. I thought of what

I'd felt, seeing the photo frame smashed like that.

Quietly, "I couldn't stand it. I can't stand it. Watching you suffer."

Val frowned. "Suffer?"

"I'd want to help you, solve a few things, care for you. And you'd feel appropriated, like your terms of living are not being respected. Like you're getting *owned* a little more each day. I don't want to own you, Val. I just can't stand it, you trying to do everything alone."

There was quiet for a while. Val's eyes still processing that, and heat edging into her face. It could be anger or something else.

Val said, "I'm not suffering, I'm struggling. If you don't know the difference, that's okay, but there is one."

"Tell me."

"Well." She thought about it. "Every day I get up in purity. Only giving my energy to what I really give a fuck about. There's no pain in that."

"Just starvation and the threat of homelessness."

She snorted. "I've never starved."

"One day to the next, you can't rule it out, though."

"But you can, in your life?"

I shrugged. Of course.

She said, "Tell me what that brings you exactly." When I was silent, "Really, Cél, tell me what it means to have the 'freedom' to faddle over quinoa."

I smiled grimly. "You always go for quinoa."

"What?"

"When you mock the middle class. For the record, I fucking hate quinoa. It's like bouffant frogspawn."

Val took a breath. "Okay." After a silence, she said, "So if I obsessed more about material shit, we'd be good together. Otherwise we're a cheese party on the Titanic."

She seemed to dislike her own sarcasm. She grabbed the unlit cigarette from behind her ear and tossed it away. Then she put her eyes on me. New concentration in them.

She said, "What would you need from me?"

The word arrived slowly. "Handholds."

She puzzled over that for a moment, but said nothing.

I said, "And you? From me?"

"See my life from the inside out. Step into the joy with me. You're still looking at it from the outside." Then she said, "Handholds?"

"Things you'd let me do for you."

Her eyes rolled. "Money?"

"Not directly."

"Indirectly, then." More eyeroll. "Cash pushed under my door in a brown envelope?"

"Sharing. Sharing in my good things."

Val swallowed, seemed to want her cigarette back. "I've got nothing to share back."

"That is…" My voice cracked at the scale of the inaccuracy. "That is not true."

"Nothing material."

"I'm talking about experiences."

"I don't –"

"I'm talking about the way you make me feel."

We looked at each other. Quite drunk suddenly. Words can do that as well.

Val's ungloved hand went to the small of my back.

"Val..." That was barely a sound. Her hand began to rise up my back. "Val... no. We can't just deal with it by..."

"Disagree." She was about to lean in with her beautiful mouth, when resistance would be –

"I don't just want you *once*," I said furiously.

Wicked smile. "Fine."

I touched her mouth to stop the kiss. "And it's your turn."

"Turn?"

"Why we wouldn't work."

After a moment, Val sighed. We moved apart, her hand leaving my back and retrieving another cigarette from her pocket. This one she lighted up.

She said, "I don't see how you'd be happy, up close to my life. I mean, I don't want red velvet anything."

I looked away, pretended this was a new thought. "Red velvet nothing."

"Yeah."

I smiled a little. "Not even cake?"

"Fine. Red velvet cake. But no little silver folk. Bare hands only. Like apes." There was unsounded laughter between us. Then Val summarized, "Red velvet fuck all." She looked at me sadly. "You couldn't do it, Cél. In bed, it wouldn't matter. Everywhere else... I'd feel poor."

"Well. As much as spending all our time in bed would

be…" I took a moment. "I want more than that. And so do you, or you'd've had me a long time ago."

She looked at me. Unhappily, it seemed, she couldn't deny it.

The Seine was now throbbing with rain. We stared through our doubts at the skyline. Getting nowhere.

I said, "We should probably get out of the rain."

"Walk me home?"

"The metro?"

"I meant that."

We walked awhile, and the metro soon came up ahead.

Val said, "I changed my mind. Walk me home. Unless the rain is bothering you?"

"I don't know where you live."

"Warehouse on Lecourbe." Before I could say anything, she added, "It's just for a few days."

With effort, I limited my remark to, "Okay."

"But we don't have to talk, right? I really didn't sleep well."

"Quiet is good. You want one of my gloves?"

Val grimaced. "No gallantry."

"Got it. Frostbite is a good look, anyhow."

She giggled. Not a sound she made often. I liked it.

"I've heard it's great for poets," I said.

"Shut up."

A few blocks later, she put her cold hand in mine.

1.

The "warehouse on rue Lecourbe" had turned out to be a derelict building wearing a fixed grin of *For Rent* signs.

As we'd walked there, Val had explained there was an (athletic, hazardous) way of getting inside the warehouse via the neighboring parking lot. When caught, the three guys who'd first infiltrated and made their home there were allowed to stay on one condition: they keep everyone else out. *By any means*, the guy who owned the warehouse had told them. He was a paunchy golfer of Cambodian descent with a thick accent, so they could pretend he'd said, *By many means*. They were a rent boy, a gig-worker in food delivery, and an ex-construction worker with bad lungs. Nice guys down on their luck, who weren't about to hurt anyone, intruder or otherwise.

They let Val stay with them when she was between "arrangements" because one of Val's cousins had been a colleague of the construction worker before he got emphysema. Val's cousin still came around sometimes, with rotisserie chicken and chocolate milk for his old friend. Val didn't feel unsafe with them because that cousin was as unforgiving as he was thoughtful. If anything happened to her, there would be what that cousin called "Algerian applause", and the perpetrator would require help from a nurse for the rest of his life.

As we parted a little way from the warehouse, Val and I had agreed to take some time apart to think about our next move. There didn't have to be certainty, but there did have to be courage. Whatever we chose, we couldn't be weak about it.

"Hmmm," Val had said and looked at my mouth very closely.

I tucked her wet hair behind her ear. "Hmmm."

We'd parted clammily like hot plastic. All my cells telegramming furiously that I was walking the wrong way.

Nine days passed. On the second of them, my firm offered me an all-expenses-paid trip to assist in a bid on a mall design contract. The destination: Los Angeles. I thought about imported palm trees and declined. I needed to be here right now, I said. A family thing.

I kept on with my life, just as it was. I snicked and sliced at architectural grids on my computer. I nodded through development meetings about co-working spaces for Gen-Zs, the decor of which had to be inspired by airplane cabins. ("For Gen-Z, that's their safe space.") Coffee shops that had to be discreetly laptop-proof. Skate parks that had to be discreet, period. Outside of work, I assembled fragrant vegan wonder-bowls and chewed them neatly during the dates I made myself continue, emceed by Pinot Grigio. I signed clipboards in the street calling for the latest rapist to resign. I flossed.

When none of that shook the feeling that something in my life had shifted, that a door was now ajar I had never before thought could open – should open – I took to walking the city for hours on end. Brushing up against stories, watching other people's choices play out in real time.

The only neighborhood I avoided was Nation. The derelict warehouse truly had been for just a few days, and Nation was where Val was living now, in her next borrowed apartment. I didn't want a chance encounter between us to disrupt our intentionality, our ownership of what came next, which felt invigorating.

When my feet got sore or the rain too aggressive, I'd duck into a branch of the library and head to Poetry. This was always a small, poky section, where scorched teenagers would be squatting with the porny or queer or housewife stuff they didn't want recorded on their library card.

My only experience of poetry so far, outside of Valérie, was school tests, weddings, and the slogan mugs of girl-friends in self-help groups. As for Valérie's poems, I'd seen a few at the house parties I'd attended early on in our friendship. No way to get through the room because of the kids on the floor with Lidl wine and 1990s boardgames. These kids were disheveled, beautiful, insecure, and courageous when united. They were the friends of Valérie's I could never quite decipher or get comfortable with.

I'd be marooned somewhere – lispy Sorbonne pansexual to the left, bicycle mechanic with neck tattoo to the right – and not seeing Val anywhere. A paper would randomly arrive, handed along by someone nearby. It was a page ripped out of a Carrefour notepad with a column of Valérie's scrawl on it, no capitalization, no punctuation, could have been a shopping list. This was how she shared her poems: exactly as they'd been written, the only copy. She would shrug it for release into the tide of party hands after a friend exclaimed this was one that should be toured. It always got back to her. Her friends made sure of it.

They were poems about nothing much. Bicycles abandoned in the street, their frames stripped by thieves then graffitied with political angst and influencer stickers. (Typically a real-life bicycle would inspire each of these poems. Val would imagine the bicycle's history, then tape to its frame a copy of the poem, unsigned. She'd take a picture, and walk away.) Coins in a fountain that addicts would steal to buy heroin. Then, when they got high, they'd have visions of what was wished for with each coin. A homeless man in Air Jordans who busked with a plastic flute by the Eiffel, then suddenly disappeared. Those were the things

Val wrote about.

I knew that I liked what I read and wanted others to like it too, so that Val could make a living from it. But, if I'm honest, I didn't know what I was looking at. It was like a bamboo souvenir from a distant country about which I knew only that things were not done there the way they were here. Challenge the recipient of such a souvenir to guess its value... and you have me, as I am with Valérie's work.

I figured a first step was to know more about poetry. So I came to the library.

Stumping through poem after poem all by myself quickly became frustrating. Many of the earliest poems in history seemed to be about the Trojan War, which a woman had caused by being too hot. I got distracted by Googling "is the trojan war real", with the search results offering plot summaries that were way more exciting than the actual poems. The less old (but still old) stuff kept name-dropping the Trojan War. Now that I knew it was fictional, and given all the real wars that had happened in the meantime, that seemed kind of weird. The concept of being oppressed by a woman's hotness continued into this period too. The oppression was particularly elevating if she had never shown the slightest bit of interest. Rather than start a war about it, these poets lolloped around, honoring leaf fall in the Lake District.

I gave up on the old stuff. Maybe modern poetry would be more honest.

I found myself struggling there as well. Modern poetry was at least written in language that didn't sound sermonic and peculiar except at weddings or graduation ceremonies, or from your drunk friend who works in theater. This was generally just normal language – the kind people truly used in their unguarded moments, that you might hear hollered across a parking lot. Some of the figures missing from history were writing now too, telling of the bruises kept out of view in the past. And, at long last, nobody gave a shit about the Trojan War.

But the hot thing in modern poetry seemed to be to take those perfectly fine, perfectly ordinary words and then neurotically shuffle them around. Like this:

> *The cat*
> *Sat on the (mat)*
> *Mat?*
> *The cat did*
> *Sat there*
> *Matting (matting matting)*
> *Ssshhh!*
> *It stands*

It drove me crazy. Artificial in another way. And yet poems like that were passionately analyzed and given glowing forewords by cultural center laureates and professors at leafy universities. These were people who knew poetry, who'd given their whole lives to it. They'd done the work of years that I was trying to do in a few wet afternoons of haphazard riffling. So, whatever it felt like to me, this was poetry.

I tried a few more times to engage with it, then I gave up. I went to a movie instead or, as spring gained confidence, stayed out in the mellowing rain. That was poetry, that was Valérie's world.

And the truth was, I just didn't get it.

If you can't understand a person's priorities, you should probably just stay the fuck away from them. Right? I drifted around the city, trying to decide if that was true.

After then, I began to head to Bagnolet in my city walks. It's possible that not understanding one part of Val's life made me curious about another.

You can drift into Bagnolet easily enough from the 20th arrondissement. Its western perimeter is the Périphérique freeway, where kids hang out on the overpass, precision-spitting at government-vibe vehicles in the traffic below, playing for Haribo and girls' phone numbers. The number '93' starts showing up, scraped into unguarded wet cement or spray-painted onto the ass of a billboard hottie. Department 93, or Saint-Seine-Denis. The poorest *département* in mainland France, where one in every three of the population is an immigrant. Valérie was born and raised here.

The Chaibi family – Hamdan, Samia, and their four girls – had lived in a three-room apartment halfway up a starkly unimaginative high-rise. It was one of several such buildings on that *cité HLM*, or low-income housing estate. There were windows that looked out onto a yard of shifting gravel piles. There were corridor wars over stolen laundry and murdered pets. There was 'tits taste titty' scratched on the lobby glass. The communal dumpsters were full of tins of condensed milk after Ramadan. As for the fire escapes, they were useless. This was on account of the Brazilians, who'd plant down a Virgin Mary statue on the stairs, whereupon it became a Catholic shrine, an impassable bramble of candles and flowers.

I'd heard all this from Val over the years. She'd left the high-rise at fifteen, but only to move to a cousin's place three blocks north. In fact, she had never in her life lived more than 12 miles from Bagnolet in Department 93.

Things for me had started very differently, in a pink-brick small town in Normandy. My father was a bargeman on the river Sarthe. My mother worked at a gift shop commemorating the region's pears. There was no money in either of their families, and their jobs did nothing to change that. My brother Thibalt and I were told to do well in school or else get really enthusiastic about pears.

Thibalt bailed on that challenge early and joined the military. I took my own sweet time to get worked up about it. For the first thirteen years of my life, I mainly tromped across orchards, 'Keep Out' registering as 'All Yours, Kiddo'. I spied on girls with ribboned bicycles who stripped off at the lake. I read Dumas and Saint-Exupéry in decrepit row-boats I'd borrowed without asking, giving myself the shits on low-hanging plums.

What changed things was a high-school trip to Paris, a stones-and-bones tour of the capital. The part I remember was the Palais Garnier, the opera house in the 9th arrondissement. There were bronze busts of composers mounted high on the building, and I noticed that every single one of them was male. The only sculptures of women were generic nymphs with their tits out. My teacher said this was because there weren't any female architects back then. So men put their own faces on buildings, and women who wanted to see their own faces were told to go look in the mirror.

A dream was born. Five years later, I was studying architecture at Paris Dauphine and interning at the firm that now employed me.

Since then, Paris had become home to me way more than Normandy ever was. All the same, I periodically needed to get the hell out of the city. I'd take the TGV train in almost any direction... Orléans, Brive-La-Gaillarde, Nice, Barcelona. To probe only 12 miles beyond where I was born, and always in Paris... I just couldn't imagine it.

I tried to, though, as I walked around Bagnolet. I pictured Valérie here, happily here.

The corner-store troupe of schoolgirls in hijabs and saris

who sucked on neon-colored ice tubes and glared at boys in annoyed interest. The pot-bellied young men astride mopeds parked across the sidewalk, yawning and smoking and tweaking their ring tones. The variety stores with heaped plastic boxes of slippers, handbags, dishware... all of it looking like it had been stolen from motels. Lefty rage sprayed or wheat-pasted or stickered everywhere. 'Eat the rich'. 'ACAB'. 'Rage hard, Fuck tender'.

As I walked around, I remembered why I never really came here.

The faces that looked back at me were pissed I'd ever forgotten. They probably thought I was a tourist from some quirky far-off whiteland like Australia. I thought about turning back to the nearest metro station and heading home, calling in at a flower shop for a mood reset.

But one thought stopped me. I knew someone formed here, on these streets. More than that, I loved her. Someone who would never walk this neighborhood with these feelings. This fear. Yes, fear.

This was Valérie's home. With a hold on her so strong that 12 miles' distance from it was the limit. There was wonderful here, there had to be. Val was no less interested in fulfilment and beauty than I was.

Led by these truths, I kept going. I came back other days too.

Over time, I discovered that Bagnolet is crusty at its western edge, by the freeway – all motels, big-box stores and self-storage. But push on north and east, and it changes. The streets get narrower, with older bones. Houses now, not tenement, with their front doors opening directly onto the sidewalks. Handwritten signs not to park in front of this rusting gate or that grilled front. Everything uneven and worn, walls with dirty ankles, shutters closed like they never opened. Spray-paint still a second skin, but more murals here, painstakingly designed and with community consent implied in their locations. Neighborhood pride a popular theme of the murals.

How calm it was. That's what I came to appreciate first. The exhausting agitation of the city felt entirely absent.

The small things charmed me next. The lopsided hoops on a community basketball court, and the tubby Asian kids in cheap eyeglasses taking improbable shots from twenty feet out. Then their dorky little glory dances and whoops from their friends in the sidelines. A chipped bathtub on a street corner, filled with soil and transformed into a flower bed. An old lady in a ramshackle electric wheelchair, stopped at random, no apparent plans to move along. Her rough white face angled into the sunshine, smoking as though post-coitally. She met my eyes incuriously, then nodded in a wordless *what's up*. I nodded back. No smile because she didn't want one. But I walked on feeling like a smile had happened.

I did not know, had never asked, the exact address of the housing estate on which Valérie had grown up. Our childhood talk never got that specific. Anyhow, Val would have known precise coordinates wouldn't mean very much to me, not in this neighborhood. So I eyed the social housing as I passed, but not too hard. It was rude to stare, and it was dumb. You didn't figure people out by peering through their chain link fences.

It was on my fourth walk around Bagnolet that I found it.

I'd arbitrarily taken a side street in hopes this would take me back west. The afternoon was draining from the sky and my feet were sore. It was reluctantly, then, that I registered there was something up ahead that might warrant a second glance. I did look, and I soon forgot about my feet.

A tired industrial building stood at the turn of the road, with a mural on its wall.

The mural was the full height and width of the building. It showed sunset in a Wild West desert, rendered in apocalyptic, nuclear colors. Real sunlight was boosting the mural colors, this being a road on a hilltop, with no buildings opposite to cast shadows. On the streets below this hill, you could probably see the mural from five or six blocks away.

Centered in the mural was a column of words.

I couldn't make them out from where I stood, so I moved closer.

They said:

Tonight, language has left us.
All our words emaciated,
Too long toured in our heads.
Nothing is so haggard as
The yearslong unsaid.
Release fills the room.
Fingertips rise to learn skin.

Stray dogs in the valley
Are yodeling at the misty
Reticence of stars, and
Persimmons die young,
Anonymous thuds in the yard,
On this night we breathe love
There is no unspeaking of.

Until we are done for now,
Spent, and in the spearmint
Glimmers arbitrarily lent
By headlamps, our tangled
New harmony hums
A few childlike heartbeats
Above sound.

A Vespa sputtered around the corner and didn't much like me standing in the middle of the road. I heard the estimate of my IQ from the rider, but I didn't move. I was pinned in place by how much I loved what I saw.

I took a few pictures on my phone, but they were not satisfying at all. The mural defied being pressed into pixels. It could only be experienced like this, in the moment.

Finally, I noticed the credits painted at the corner of the mural:

Paint: @Raferaw93. Words: Valérie Chaibi.

Right in the chest. I read it again, suspecting myself. Projecting her name everywhere.

No mistake. Valérie wrote this.

Minutes tiptoed by. The sun slid behind a cloud, and the apocalyptic tone of the mural deepened with the dip in light.

The date alongside the credits was February 2015. Four years ago. A few months before we'd met.

Multi-media poet.

So this is what that meant.

I couldn't say how long I stood there in the end. Time was no measure of the things that moved in me. Collapsed in me, mainly. The colossal crush and release of realizing I was wrong. I had looked for poetry only in libraries.

Walking away, I was not the same.

2.

Rue de La Galaxie. Avenue Jean Jaurès. Rue Marguerite
Yourcenar. Across derelict fencing in the Parc des
Beaumonts. On almost every wall of a former gas station in
Pantin.

Now that I knew I was looking for poetry embedded in a
mural, I found Val's work all over. Or, at least, in enough
places that it felt likely I would encounter more of it if I just
kept walking.

I took my Leica M6 with me as I searched. I put electric
tape over the brand, because my all-terrain energy for this
was taking me into streets whose anger was obvious and
limits I didn't know. There was no doubt about it: a photograph simply could not rival the experience of standing in
front of the work. All the same, I wanted something to take
with me from each mural. I thought about this irrationality
often. I don't think it was to do with memory. I think it was
wanting to make what I saw a little bit *mine*.

Within a week I had found five more murals in the three

communes immediately around Bagnolet. All of them were on buildings that must have consented to this treatment. (Heartwarming, sure, but also troubling: in a consensual arrangement, oughtn't Valérie and the artist to be paid?) The artist Val worked with changed from mural to mural, but the energy was always the same: jagged, disruptive, futuristic. The kind of colors you'd see in a computer more than in nature. Against the putty hues of these neighborhoods, they stood out from several blocks away.

The poems were all song-like, quietly euphoric or defiant, a softly stretching tide of feeling that edged up on you from out of a wall. I wondered how many people took the time to read them. I understood why these words might not change Val's future, even if once read they were not easily forgotten. How do you commercialize words on a public wall?

The sixth mural I found was for Adama Traoré, a name well-known in Paris. He was Black, young, and male. Rather, he had been. Having that precise combination of identities in France, Val's poem proposed, is why it was no surprise that Adama was now also dead.

It happened three years ago, in Val d'Oise, some fifteen miles north of this mural in Bagnolet. Gendarmes had stopped Adama and his brother to check their identity cards, and, not having his with him – a crime – Adama had sprinted off. The gendarmes gave chase, three of them ultimately pinning Adama down to the ground as they arrested him. A few hours later, Adama stopped breathing.

The state's medical report was confident that the crush of the three officers had not caused Adama's death. An independent autopsy commissioned by his family concluded the opposite.

The mural for Adama was a portrait of him, dapper in white blazer and blue shirt, sunglasses propped on his head. Val's poem was titled *Val d'Os*. Valley of Bones.

I didn't take a picture of that mural. It didn't feel right.

On the train home I made wacky faces at a Black baby and hoped he would grow up knowing there were people who believed he was who he said he was.

I developed my pictures of the murals myself, at work.

Clients with confidential briefs didn't want pictures of their projects leaking to third parties. Main-street photo developers were therefore out of the question. *Dassonville, Fabre et Hugo Architectes* mainly got around this by keeping everything digital. But some clients were seriously fucking paranoid, or seriously fucking twee, and wanted physical prints. For this reason, we had our own dark-room. It was poky and basic, but workable enough.

Staff were free to use the dark-room for personal projects, so long as this was outside office hours and the honor jar got a little something for the materials consumed.

I'd learned photo development in college and done

nothing much with it ever since. I felt my old passion stir in me again, developing the pictures of Valérie's murals. Agitating the blix, eyeballing test strips, tweaking magenta then yellow... these were rituals I loved. To center Val's work in them felt good.

Hanging up the prints to dry, I took a moment to savor this private exhibition of them, the only display they'd ever have. Beyond this room, they'd be going in a folder and then into a drawer. I couldn't put them up on a wall. They weren't mine enough for that.

When one of us had a firm feeling about our future, she would call the other. That's what Val and I had agreed, parting by the warehouse. Two weeks of silence became three. I wasn't worried. In a way, I was reassured. Val and I didn't hurry in anything. Certainly we ought not to break from that for this.

One night, floating a little on wine and Aretha Franklin, I took out my folder of the mural prints and spread them across my kitchen table. My pad was nearby, still open from a concept sketch I'd made during a client call. I pulled the pad closer and began to draw. This was the stiff, informative drawing I'd learned in my late teens, after a geometry teacher insisted there was no way to make buildings without first making sketch lines.

Don't think of it as art if that intimidates you, he'd said. Nobody wants you to bring feeling to this, any more than they want that from a pilot. (*I am a pilot*, I'd written in self-reminder at the top of my first sketchpad.)

That night, with the mural prints and my pad, I was not a pilot. I brought feeling.

I imagined a building whose interior walls were the permanent home of Val's murals. (Not the prints of the murals. The murals themselves, painted directly onto the walls.)

Each mural had its own room, which was the full height of the building – the only ceiling in this place was the roof. Some of the murals occupied only a single wall, the way I'd seen them; others I imagined expanding outward and wrapping around multiple walls of the room. Understanding that the murals were created in and for natural light, I thought about the number and position of windows, and how the light distribution would shift throughout the day, with the character of the mural shifting too.

The room for the Adama Traoré mural had no windows, or light of any kind. To see him, you had to want to – you must bring light yourself. A reminder that his story could so easily be lost to the dark without people determined to keep it alive.

Each mural room is accessed from a central hallway running from the front door to the back. There's a skylight above the hallway, matching its width exactly, and its walls and floor are mahogany. No furniture, just pure hallway.

Footlights at the base of the hallway walls power on softly when daylight fades, vertically mirroring the soft froth of a few stars above. The back door is sliding glass, then it's three or four steps down to water. A lake, I think. Valérie is on the steps, smoking. Turning when somehow she hears my footsteps, even though I was barefoot in the hall and am barefoot now on these steps. They are smooth, seasoned stone and still hold some of the warmth of the day. We sit by the lapping of the water.

I worked on the plans for two weeks. Late nights of soft jazz and sure penciling in which I remembered who I wanted to be.

It had begun with imagining a home for Val's work. Very soon what I was imagining was a home for us.

What broke our silence was the seventh mural I found.

There'd been a run of exuberantly sunny days, unusual for March. My fellow Parisians celebrated with a citywide protest against the cost of living.

The offices of *Dassonville, Fabre et Hugo Architectes* were just off the Place de la République, where protests typically began or ended. (Many of them about Algeria. Nearly every weekend, in fact, the Place de la République saw its Marianne statue involuntarily wield the Algerian flag, as French-Algerians refused to let the Republic lipstick the past. Valérie – looking at the floor and never with her family around – would admit she'd chosen not to think about it. She had enough problems, she said, just in the things she could potentially do something about. Add to her spatial sense of the world the problems that came with her *ancestry* and she wouldn't see the point in even getting out of bed. This French-Algerian, Val said, would get back at France by succeeding in it.)

Today's protest was particularly fierce. The streets around République were full of citizen journalists touting video phones, and limping cops with smashed visors. On account of the disruption, I'd been given permission to clock off early and finish up at home. I went instead to the calm I'd noted in Seine-Saint-Denis.

My wanderings this time took me to Les Lilas. This was a neighborhood at the northern end of the Rue de Belleville, immediately outside the city perimeter. Lilas had more than its fair share of Halal chicken, unschooled artists, and roadworks. It also had more than its fair share of people, period, many of them congregating glumly on the sidewalks like they were waiting to be allowed back inside after a fire drill. The energy was young, broke, restless.

The mural I found in Lilas was on the side of a former ink

factory. The ink brand was high on the wall in faded paint, and the mural responded to it, using the same pastel colors and rigid geometry. The entire piece had then been scrubbed and thinned to look aged too.

The mural showed a field with workers scattered across it, stooped and sun-hatted. They were pulling words from the earth, as they might pull potatoes, with some of the words trailing roots and clods of soil. A worker in the foreground had paused with an uprooted word in his hand and was looking across at a citadel on the skyline. These were broad-stroked figures, so he had no face – nothing to tell us what he was feeling as he looked. But his posture, and the way he was twisting to see the citadel, was wistful. The word in his hand was "Elysian".

This was Val's poem:

> *When I bruise, may I bruise vividly.*
> *Show me that flesh is soft and the spirit*
> *Loose, but that tested life leaves color.*
>
> *When I lose, take everything, leave me*
> *Derelict. Prove all foundations figments.*
> *In that pit of need may I learn what I am.*
>
> *Let me be mad, if in that unarmoring I may*
> *Run with synaptic grace and with my*
> *Full face witness the domain of the sun.*

Give me feelings that are not yet named.
Have textbooks omit me, committees not
Permit me. Let me be the future early.

I will yearn, reach always across the flame.
Let me. Should I have accomplices, may I trust
Wisely or forgive without gnawing regret.

Have me love. Love: the living inside living.
May I love from my fractures, the jagged edges
I thought unsafe. Love, have me.

Let me love while I live and live while I dream.
But let me dream, oh hear this: let me dream.
Have it forever scream in my bones, the world

The other side of refusal to compromise.
To pastel simpering ease: I will not concede.
My eyes are higher, on my heart's misty spire.

Below this was written: *In memory of Fabrice Gelenbe, February 17 1991 - April 4 2016.*

Fabrice. Val's friend, the "novelist". The one who'd killed himself.

In the mural, I took in again the worker turned toward the citadel, grateful suddenly that he didn't have a face. I understood it too: Fabrice had hated having his photograph taken. He wasn't bad-looking, and could get a girl easily enough. But he had, I think, an extreme aversion to being judged. If you looked at him too long, he was unnerved and would glare at you. A photograph enabled someone to look at him indefinitely. Of course he didn't like having his picture taken.

It had been a while since I'd thought about Fabrice. I stood by the mural and let him back into my head.

The truth was, I'd never gotten along with him. His choice to die had not prompted in me a grand reimagining of him.

It had scared me, though. Fabrice had been so sure of himself and his purpose. A writer whose stories would stretch above his jagged beginnings in the Marseille projects and touch the universal. That was his destiny, he said. Bitterly said. Half the time, he seemed to loathe it, to wish it wasn't true. Far from a choice, it was the destroyer of choice, life-limiting, embedded in him like shrapnel.

These were the agitations Fabrice expressed at great length to the small circle of friends who could stand it. Potheads, mainly, but also a few brittles and strays who liked the idea that talent could be crippling and destiny a chokehold. That dignified their own positions, whether they were struggling or not trying at all. Potheads, brittles, strays... and Valérie. She'd sit there looking restless and unconvinced, but that didn't seem to bother Fab or, for that matter, Valérie. She still sat there.

They'd met at a fuel tax protest in Montreuil when Fabrice was sixteen and – bored, experimentally – Val had claimed the same. When Fabrice eventually learned Val was three years older (it took a while), he'd laughed at how completely, and pointlessly, she'd fooled him. They'd had a high tolerance for each other's bullshit ever since.

The only time Val had ever spoken to me about Fabrice's death, she'd said, "There was a gap. A gap, and it became an abyss."

"An honesty gap maybe?" I said slightly, wondering if this was reckless.

"Not that." Val looked away, then turned back sharply with, "Honest with who?"

"I mean, all those times he was talking it up, but –"

"Never mind, Cél. Okay? Just forget it." We both tried to do just that, but very soon, with a horrified laugh, Val said, "What he did in the end. Wouldn't you call that honest?"

"I meant in his –"

"Never mind. Never mind."

Frankly, I saw a great many gaps. For instance, while Val worked hard to be a good tenant in her "arrangements", understanding that her survival depended on it, Fab seemed to think himself entitled to support. He'd demand a spare room from a sister or an ex, then hammer at his cheap, stiff keyboard all times of the day and night. (Typing what exactly will never be known; he'd wiped his hard drive the night before he died.) He'd fry up entire ten-packs of quick-sale pork chops, then stack them bareback in the fridge for future consumption. He'd make a partial contribution to the utility bills, according to his (fantastical) calculation of what he'd consumed. No sister or ex could take it for more than a few weeks.

When he was asked to leave, there'd be stunned fury and intensely quiet packing. Then Fab would tape the key to their front door with FOUNT OF HUMAN KINDNESS scrawled across the wood below in Sharpie. Sometimes this defacement would cost the sister or ex their deposit.

In other words, Fabrice repelled the very people who might have made a creative life economically possible for him. Because he was a prick, rent became unavoidable. That meant a full-time job, which meant almost no time left for writing.

Toward the end of his life, on those days he didn't write, which was most days, Fab was morose and vicious, snorting more often than speaking. He'd sprawl in a perimeter chair with his legs jutting out, inconveniencing new arrivals and departees. No one said a thing, just edged around him with smile-shape mouth and skittish eyes. I could imagine him hurting someone when he was like that. What I had never imagined, not in a million years, was Fabrice hurting himself.

And *how* he'd hurt himself. At a level crossing in Châtillon-la-Borde, he'd driven onto the tracks and waited for the TGV train. Footage from a nearby security camera showed Fabrice fiddling with the dashboard radio, lighting a cigarette, staring into the rain jouncing off the hood of the car.

Châtillon was 42 miles outside of Paris: he'd driven for an hour to get there. After his death, his browser history revealed he'd picked this level crossing after painstakingly reviewing his options via street view in Google Maps. Even the car he was in had taken pre-meditation: he didn't own one himself, and so for two months had eaten only one meal a day to save up the rental fees. Nobody could comfort themselves that his death had been a rash act in a down-swing of mood.

"How is it that some people," a friend of his had said, "Dream themselves to death?"

This was at the gathering Val had organized by the Canal Saint-Martin, the night after Fab's death. The French media were marveling not at the fact he had killed himself, but that he hadn't killed anyone else. (Six passengers were taken to the hospital with bruising from the driver's attempt to stop. The driver himself was undergoing psych treatment.) The Minister of the Interior told *Le Monde* that Fabrice's choices continued a pattern of broken young men whose contempt for their own life becomes indistinguish-able from contempt for the lives of others. One commentator even referred to the Germanwings pilot who the year before had included 149 other people in his suicide crash into the French Alps.

There was anger, then, in this gathering by the canal. The villainy poured on Fabrice seemed only to confirm to them that there had never been a foothold for him in this world, which meant, at least to some of them, none for them either. Their refusal to acknowledge the simple physics of it – that the impact ought, by rights, to have derailed the train and killed no small number of passengers – is why it was the last gathering of this particular group I ever attended.

But the soft, lost voice in which that question had been offered into the silence – *How is it that some people dream themselves to death?* – stayed with me. I could barely make out the speaker, he was just a profile in the dark. Who he was didn't matter. It was the shiver that passed through for a moment – through all of them and through me too. There was no way not to dream. You could only hope that dreaming was kind to you.

In my photo records, I titled the Fabrice mural *Elysian*. I returned to it several times over the following week. On my last visit, I read those words again:

In memory of Fabrice Gelenbe, February 17 1991 - April 4 2016.

April 4th.

And I knew what I had to do. Wanted to do. I knew.

3.

On the anniversary of his death, friends of Fabrice always met at that same spot by Canal Saint-Martin where they'd gathered that first night. One of the rituals of this gathering had begun that first time too: a bottle of vodka passed around, each person taking a swig then spitting it back out into the water. A rejection of intoxication, a commitment to staying alert to things as they really were.

Valérie never missed this gathering. Nor did Fabrice's girlfriend, who'd secretly aborted his baby a few months before he died and now felt those evacuated cells like a limb she'd cut from herself when drunk. There were also Fabrice's roommates in Belleville, all of them variations on mostly benign stoner with no money. One made parkour videos; one fried chicken in a street-truck; one edited Wikipedia while waiting for his unemployment check. There were a few women from the *collage féministe* street-art collective for which Fabrice sometimes wrote slogans. Finally, there was the editor of the underground literary zine that had published excerpts from the works Fabrice was struggling to turn into a novel. These were the people who showed up, year after year.

They all still declared their relationship to Fabrice in the present-tense: girlfriend, for example, not ex-girlfriend. Perhaps because you become "ex" through mutual severance. With Fabrice it had been entirely one-sided.

They met at 9pm where the canal curved a little to the east, a few blocks from the Gare de l'Est. The canalside here was cobbled and put their butts to sleep – their backs if they lay down, as some of them did. But this was tolerated because the lights of nearby buildings did not quite reach this curve, so they could hide their feelings in the dark.

The editor would read aloud Fabrice's work, his Quebecois accent undulating in ways that could still take them all by surprise. Then there would be speeches for Fabrice from the others, sometimes prepared, sometimes spontaneous. For some of them, this would be the first time they'd allowed themselves to check in with their feelings since the last anniversary. That's just how they got through it. Valérie, I think, was one of those people.

After the speeches came the vodka ritual: spitting it out into the water. Then, in conclusion of the gathering, there'd be silence. There was no prescribed length to this silence. When a person felt that participating in it any longer would be dishonest, they got up and left without acknowledging anyone else. The girlfriend was always the last to leave. Val was generally second-to-last, touching the nearly drained vodka bottle to the girlfriend's shoulder as she went. The last few mouthfuls in the bottle, Val knew, the girlfriend always drank, just as soon as there was no one else around to witness it.

On this April 4th, I arrived by the canal at 9pm exactly. I was very sure of that. All the same, the gathering was already underway, the editor reading aloud Fabrice's work. They must have changed the time this year.

The attendees I considered typical were all there. There were a few other faces too, some that pressed on memories in me but too faintly for their name or story to spring up. They were sitting in a rough circle, mostly looking at their hands, their shoes, the skyline. Val was sidelong to me, gazing into the smudge of lights on the water. Wearing the red cashmere sweater, of course.

There was no way I was shoving myself into a largely solid circle like that. A bench a little way off was still within earshot of them. I sat there instead and listened in, my head at an angle that wasn't quite watching. My approach had not registered with any of them above the noise of passing traffic or in the thin light from the nearest streetlamp. They were all absorbed in Fabrice's writing.

Fabrice's writing… I struggled with it. It was very obvious he spent a lot of time with words. He would endlessly twist them around and in on themselves, arrangements you couldn't probe too much or they'd fall apart. I'm just not sure that's what a story is.

The excerpt the editor was sharing tonight was a

first-person narrative written by the wind as it swept the earth. The wind, being immortal, had seen many thousands of years of growth and disintegration. But the present treatment of the planet by capitalist human society had the wind wishing it could carry fire so that it incinerated whatever it touched. It didn't want to witness this anymore.

The piece might resonate with some people, but its relish in vengeful mass destruction turned me off. I stopped trying to engage with the words. Instead I let them work on me as low, uninterrupted sound, like muffled shipping news from a neighbor's radio. When the editor finished and my eyes returned from staring into a not unpleasant sort of nothing, I saw that Valérie had noticed me.

Surprise seemed to be ebbing out of her face – she'd been aware of me for a while. What that left in her expression... well, she wasn't displeased. Whatever her feelings were exactly, though, there was nervousness around the edges. I didn't want that, so I arranged myself more loosely on the bench and tried to make my eyes steadily absorbent with no needs in them. I wasn't here for something from Valérie. I was defining something for myself.

A few of the others had followed Val's look and noticed me too. But it had been three years since most of them had seen me. My hairstyle had changed, and I'd gotten richer. So recognition either didn't happen or wasn't emotionally significant to anyone but Val.

Now they took turns to speak about Fabrice. Those who wanted to, at least, which was about one in every three.

The Belleville roommates had become more expressive since I'd last heard them. They laughingly recalled Fabrice's weird waste disposal habits, and described the video game the Wikipedia editor was presently coding, based on an idea Fabrice had during one of their midnight smokes.

The girlfriend put out a few ragged sentences about the clock sounding like something infinitely dripping. A few others talked about their grief being a limp, or a bird that stared in through the breakfast window, or the redundant number never deleted from their phone. Their speeches had a borrowed, recited feel, though. Fab had been dead three years, and the current of time was smoothing this flint to a pebble, it seemed. Even the zine editor was restless. The speech he gave – about true talent condemned to vagrancy in a capitalist world of "attention exploitation" – could have been a complaint for himself more than for Fabrice.

Val's turn to speak arrived. She took a minute. When the words did come, it was with tenderness and finality, and I thought perhaps that was the work she'd had to do in the meantime: pulling them both into her voice together, in the right proportions.

She said, "Fab. I want to let you sleep now."

There was a shift among the others as they realized that was it, nothing more was coming. The girlfriend in particular seemed still to be weighing those words, and not happily, when Val motioned to the vodka in suggestion they move on to the next part of their ritual. One of the roommates got to his feet in agreement.

In grim silence, each of them approached the water, accepted the bottle from the previous person, then spat vodka into the canal.

When I'd witnessed this the first time, three years ago, my skin had crawled. So teenage and contrived. In our talk about the gathering afterward, Val had sensed my disdain and rolled her eyes.

She'd said, "Because tucking them in the ground to rot, sad songs playing they cannot hear? Isn't weird *at all*? It's death. There's no sane way of dealing with it."

Tonight, after Val had her turn with the vodka, she kept the bottle in her hand and looked at me. Her meaning was clear. Was I going to truly show up?

Shit. I looked away, wanting the night to fold in over me, make me invisible. I'd come here to be part of this, but not in the way she was asking.

The silence from the group took on an edge as Val stood there, waiting for me to do something. I looked back and saw most heads were turned toward me now, some annoyed or bemused.

Spitting vodka? While they all watched? That belonged in the same universe as me giving a speech about Fabrice. Or me sharing a blunt with Fabrice on a warehouse-party rooftop, while he talked about the tense in the Turkish language that was used exclusively for hearsay. How his father had urged him to live ravenously, so that he never had to use that tense because everything he spoke of was direct experience. I'd been behind Valérie and Fab on the rooftop when they'd had that conversation, and I'd understood for the first time what I could never have with them – with Valérie – as a daughter only of France.

Finally, my hands answered. I motioned at Val, maybe a little angrily. *No.*

Val shrugged and handed the vodka bottle along to the next person. She flapped a hand at the girlfriend and the others who were confused by the delay: never mind, it's nothing. She must have forgotten what a terrible fit we were in a group.

I felt ridiculous suddenly, being here, thinking I could ever be part of it. I should probably just leave.

Valérie must have sensed that's where my thoughts were leaning, because, as she sat down again, she shot me a look that said: stay.

Now it was the final silence, when the group would wordlessly disperse, each leaving at the time that felt right to them. Tonight the editor left first, then the feminist street-artists, then some of the faces I had no names for. None of them showing me any interest as they passed.

To everyone's surprise, Valérie stood up next. Again, the girlfriend flashed confusion and unease, and her eyes moved to me accusingly. I avoided the girlfriend's look, feeling guilty on reflex even though I was sure it wasn't warranted. Val wasn't doing things differently tonight because I was here. That's just not who she was.

In a few strides Val was by me and motioning with her head: let's go.

We walked south, the canal passing through a lock alongside us as it crossed the Square des Récollets. The night cafés were loading the breeze with blended chatter and cigarette smoke, and not far off a bell was tolling ambiguously: it could be for happy reasons or sad.

Val said, "Guess you don't spit, huh, princess."

"You know I don't."

"I also know you don't come out for Fabrice. Tonight you did. Tonight you're different."

I said, "Not that different."

She looked at me for a moment. "Good. I don't want you that different."

"No?"

"Changing yourself for someone else, that's just fucken doomed."

We came to a mutual halt in our ambling and almost faced each other. Val looked tired and shaken, her eyes meeting mine only briefly before drifting off.

I said, "You okay?"

She shrugged. "Always a weird night."

"Yeah."

"Fabrice..." She thought about him. "He's had a lot of my feelings for a long time. And I'm okay with that. It's kept him around. But now…" Almost immediately, guilt seemed to nip her. "I mean, I'll always show up for this night, to remember him, I just –"

"Val. It's okay."

She looked at the hand I'd darted out to comfort her. On the arm of the red sweater.

"I want to feel other things now." She said that quietly, studying me.

After a silence, she said, "Why did you come?"

"Step into the joy, you said. The joy of what you do. See your life from the inside out."

"Yes."

"Not just the joy, Val. All of it."

She was shy suddenly, and picked at her sleeve. "And how are you so sure that's what you want?"

"Would it be enough to say, there was work I had to do, and I've done it?"

Her eyes came back to me. New interest in them. But still… so tired. Not tired how she'd been last time, when she hadn't slept. Another kind of tired.

On a hunch I said, "Has something happened?"

She cocked her head as though to marvel at that. Grimly, "Yeah… I guess the 16th arrondissement hasn't heard yet."

"Heard?"

"They killed another one. The gendarmes. In Clichy-sous-Bois."

"Another…" I found myself in a language dead-end. No way was I saying *young Black male*.

"Human," Val said.

"Was he..."

"What?"

"Armed or something?"

Val turned away from me, her face hardening. "I tell you they kill him. And the first thought you have is not how violent they are, it's that maybe *he* was."

Shit. I felt my face burning up. "I'm sorry."

"Is that your France? Wait to hear if the kid was kind to animals before you condemn state execution?"

"No. No, it isn't. Val, come on. I'm sorry."

I put both my hands on her, to stabilize the moment, which seemed to be wildly keeling. She grabbed at me too, in anger, and the result of the impromptu force on both sides was – close. We were suddenly very close.

Our faces had never been closer, in fact.

It was excruciating for a moment. There was nowhere to look but her eyes. I watched her pupils dilate in the shadow cast by my sudden proximity. The disappointment in them took longer to shift.

I said, "I'm working on how I think about things. I might need a little patience."

A few strands of her hair tickled my face in a surge of the breeze. The trees by us murmured with it too. Then Val touched her forehead to mine.

Her breath warmed my lips as she said, "That's what we were asking each other, no? To work on things, things we already know we could do better."

She had a tilde-shaped scar, a few millimeters long, just above her left cheekbone. If she'd told me the story behind it, I'd forgotten. Her eyes watched me observe it, and seemed to like my curiosity. Then she dabbed her fingertip to my mouth, such a slight touch, and pulled back.

She said, "I have to go. There's a protest for Altan, the kid they killed. It's why we started early for Fabrice."

"Protest?" My instinct was dismay, but I tamped it down. I took a breath. "Where?"

"Île de la Cité."

The tiny island between the Left Bank and the Right. I toured it in my imagination for a moment. "The police building?"

"Of course."

"At night? You'd get way more media coverage in the morning."

"Fireworks." Val closed her eyes, seemed to step into the scene in her imagination. "The kid they killed was throwing fireworks. That's why the gendarmes went after him. Then he – he's cornered in an alleyway, rolling dumpsters at them. He reaches inside a dumpster, maybe for something to throw, I don't know. And that's when they shoot him." She opened her eyes. "So that's what we're taking to the police. Fireworks."

I couldn't keep it down anymore. "No, Val. Fireworks?"

She broke eye contact. "It's what the moment demands."

"Someone gets hurt. That's a guarantee."

"Someone already got hurt."

"Listen to me. Fireworks, that's explosives. Explosives set off near a government building? You know they'll jump on a terrorism protocol for that."

"You're a lawyer now?"

"I'm someone familiar with our government, and how it handles in-person criticism from social minorities. You're familiar with it too. Don't go."

Val muttered, "Fuck's sake..." But doubt had crept into her voice. She heard it herself and was infuriated. "When have the police ever chased you through the streets, Cél? One time, and I won't go."

"We're not in disagreement about the injustice. It's what you're going to do about it that –"

"You have the luxury of multiple choices, what to do about it. I don't."

"Not true. Your choices are as luxurious as your imagination, and I hardly think I beat you there."

There was a split-second of confusion over that, then Val snorted it away. "You can dismiss protest because it's never been your only resort. I mean, have you ever protested? Even once?"

I looked back at her bluntly. She already knew the answer, but here's what I knew: irrelevant.

I said, "Right now you hate the state –"

"Right now? You think it's a *phase*?"

"Indefinitely, then. That's every reason not to give the state a piece of your life. France will own you in prison –"

"Such exaggeration. Prison? Fuck that. I'll get a few –"

"You're protesting *injustice*, but figure they'll be fair when they arrest you?"

She had no comeback for that.

"Prison," I said firmly. "You won't eat until France says so. You'll feel sunshine on your face only when France says you can. France will pre-approve your toothpaste, your shoelaces, the volume on your fucking radio. And poetry? You think you'll get the time and space to –"

She put her hands over her ears. "Seriously. Just –"

"Don't go to the protest. Forget about real fireworks."

"*Shut the fuck up*, Cél."

I did not. "Have one of your artists paint fireworks on a wall instead. And the poem you write, put it right there in the middle of the explosion. Paint it over and over, multiple places around the city. So they can't turn away from one copy without turning toward another. It'll be your best piece yet."

Val had frozen in soft confusion. "What?"

Heat crossed my face as I realized I'd spoken beyond our shared limits. But the blush was gone soon. The discovery had been such a happy one, I couldn't regret it.

"I found you," I said. "On the walls. Seine-Saint-Denis."

She needed a moment with that. "For work? You went up there for work?"

I considered making an excuse. But I was tired of dishonesty. So tired of it.

I said, "You've never taken me up there. I was curious."

She repeated that last word to herself, as though she

might decipher it better in her own voice.

I said, "I wish you'd... I wish I'd seen your work sooner. But I get it. How you might think I wouldn't see it for what it is."

After a moment, "And what is that."

"Something I want in my world." I thought about my drawings. "To keep in the world."

"Keeping." Val smiled, fondly but sadly. "Not everything is about keeping."

Traditionally, this kind of talk, I'd let her have the final word. The struggling artist. The real artist. I felt the soft tug of that tradition for a moment.

Then I said, "It isn't. Probably that's what's so beautiful about wall art. No guarantee it'll still be there when you come back around again."

"Hmmm. Well, they're illegal, some of them. Repeat offending too. That's also prison time, by the way."

"Ha. Okay." I thought about my drawings again, the space I'd imagined for her work. "But they're only illegal because it has been undemocratically decided they're not worthy of space, worthy of care."

The night breeze was going at her hair again. The look she gave me through the wild scrawls of it was cautiously wondering. "Okay."

"And that's it, Val, that's where... Well, I think I've made peace with it. With how... I fit." I motioned between us. "And I think you should too."

"Fit?"

"Do you know that some of the most beautiful architecture in the world is art galleries? And libraries, and concert halls. Buildings where we keep beautiful things safe. Because the truth is, keeping safe what is beautiful, caring for it... It's as natural and right as creating those things in the first place. And art needs that. Artists... need that."

I took her hand, hard between mine. "Don't go to the protest. Stay with me."

There was quiet and stillness between us.

Then Val pulled her hand back, out of mine.

She took off the red sweater, swung it around my shoulders, and tied the arms across my mouth.

"*Mwat...*" I laughed, and tugged down the fabric to unmuffle myself. "What are you doing?"

"It's so I can't change my mind. I'd never run off without that sweater."

We were both shy suddenly. I repositioned the sweater arms to around my neck.

I said, "You're staying?"

Val gave a little smile at the stupid question and started walking again.

After a while, she said, "So what do you want to do?"

"What do you usually do? After Fab's memorial."

Val looked down the canal and thought about it. She laughed, "I'm not sure you'd be okay with it."

"Oh boy. Is it throwing quinoa at Macron?"

"No. That's Tuesdays."

"Is it dancing?" I did robot arms. "*Meep meep meepmeep meep.*"

"You know, there's still Wanted posters out for you from the last time you did that."

"Oh." I tugged on her hand. "What is it? I bet it's something I could –"

Valérie broke into a run. I stared after her.

I motioned at the sweater around my neck. "I thought you said you *weren't* going to –"

"Run!" she yelled without looking back. "I run. Fab loved to run."

She was following the canal, within tripping distance of the water. The cobblestones were dry on this mild night – all the same, I was careful. Val was not careful at all. For a while, this kept her ahead of me.

Once I caught up, I said, "Run where?"

"Doesn't matter. 'Til you can't anymore."

"Fabrice liked to run?"

She laughed at my surprise. "I know, I know! Who'd have thought?" She was breathless already, but kept yelling. "It's our original power, Cél! Wolf energy! Animals, we're fucking animals! And that's fine! Run!"

She was getting sloppy now, feet landing any old how, lurching a few times when her toe snagged. I started planning how I was going to extract her from the canal. At least until I stopped thinking altogether, which happened not long afterward.

At Square Frédérick-Lemaître, the canal went

underground beyond *Access Forbidden* signs. We carried on along the sidewalk instead, crossing the Rue du Faubourg du Temple into Square Jules Ferry, where Val came to a halt in front of the park's welcoming statue. This was of a young woman, a Grisette, which back in the 19th century meant a factory-worker who endured long hours of drudgery for almost no pay. Many Grisettes supplemented their income with sex work, but the statue didn't get into that.

Val imitated the Grisette's posture – carrying flowers in her rolled-up skirt – then bent double to recover her breath.

"By the way," she said, "I got my job back."

"Hey. What?"

But Val was running again. Her body nowhere near ready to resume, but that's what she'd decided to do. Which meant I was running again too.

She finally quit at the bandstand on the Richard Lenoir promenade. She went at its steps and sat down, very nearly broken by the rampage of these past few minutes. I did the same, one step lower owing to a toppled Lime scooter.

"You were right," she said, when she could speak at all. "I do love that job. My feelings are all I've got, so I have to be careful where I put them. But I do..." She let a beat of silence fall. "I do."

For a while, there was only the baby pinch of the night air on our skin and the sound of our breath slowly calming. The branches above us put a thick black cobweb across our view of the sky.

"Sometimes this is all I like to feel," Val said, motioning around vaguely.

I didn't ask her to explain. I think I got it.

Part Four

BOIS DE BOULOGNE

Val texted the following weekend, suggesting we meet at the Bois de Boulogne, the park near my apartment.

Me: *When*

Val: *Witching hour*

That meant 1pm, the hour at which all the idle housewives of the 16th arrondissement would jog the lakeside pathways of the park with baby-transit contraptions, side by side, wishing stock market calamities on their more radiant friends. Although I knew no women like that, they all seemed to duly emerge whenever Val was around. Or maybe it was only with her that I noticed them.

As we'd limped to the metro from our run along the Richard Lenoir promenade, Val had told me how she'd gotten her job back at the Père Lachaise cemetery. With no idea what kind of lie would succeed, she'd resorted to the truth. She wasn't used to liking a job, she told her former boss, so she'd freaked out and quit.

Her boss had needed a minute, his hands tweaking the already quite linear arrangement of annotated mail on his desk while he thought about it. Then he'd burst into laughter.

As that was the worst excuse he'd ever heard, he said, he could only assume it was the truth. His question was: How could they be sure Valérie wouldn't come to unbearably like the job again and quit a second time?

Val had described to him the learning she was presently doing: how to care about multiple things across her life simultaneously. As with all learning, she said, there would be mistakes. She just didn't think there would be the same mistake twice.

He'd absorbed that with a long, slow nod. Then he'd taken her back, at full pay, in the spirit of second chances.

It was Val's first taste of forgiveness in a long time. There had been none from the City of Paris Library: a pardon had never arrived, in the mail or otherwise. Reflecting on the karma of it – that she had probably earned her rehiring by enduring the library – Val accepted things as they were, and every month set aside ten euros from her paycheck toward the bill for the books. She would have cleared the debt in about a year and a half.

She was now living in the garage of a high school friend who used the space by day for his leather jacket business. Her first night there, Val had tried to find the bathroom in the dark and found herself groping mannequins, whose positions changed daily with his work. After our run along Richard Lenoir, Val had returned to that garage and softly played The Seekers on her friend's workbench stereo. Not understanding the English, she'd imagined French lyrics that fit the mood instead. Like these:

> *The footprints you left from my door*
> *Filled with rain, held the streetlight six hours*
> *more.*

She told me about this by text the next day, marveling at it. A quick-start on a poem, courtesy of a foreign pop-song.

That had never happened before.

Arriving at the Bois de Boulogne park, I saw Val had a dog with her today. It was a tiny, terrified thing that looked like laundry fluff had grown legs. Val explained the dog as "Schmitty's", but Schmitty had community service this week. I nodded happily, no idea who that was. I took the leash when she offered it. The dog quivered along with us as we headed toward Lake Superior.

We found a bench by the water. Our only company in sight was a kid tugging at reclusive earthworms in the grass.

Val said, "How have you been?"

"Good." I gestured vaguely. "Present. And you? How's Héloise and Abélard?"

"Still dead."

"Probably for the best."

"I don't know," Val said. "I kind of want him to show up and meet MeToo."

Héloise and Abélard were the oldest identified bones at the Père Lachaise cemetery, dating back to the twelfth century. They were also its most famous couple buried together. It was only with the revised standards championed by #MeToo in France that their love story was recognized as... problematic. Specifically, Abélard had been twenty-one years older than Héloise and seduced her after moving into her home to be her tutor. At France's pace of progress, it would probably be another fifty years before a tractor went in there and extracted Abélard, though.

"So..." Val shifted and looked pained for a moment. "You were right about the fireworks."

"Well... I don't feel great about it."

After Fabrice's memorial, the protest had gone ahead outside the police headquarters on the Île de la Cité. Eighty three protestors had been arrested, and twenty seven of them now faced criminal charges. Those captured by security camera setting off fireworks were looking at charges of terrorism, attempted assault of officers of the law, and crimes against public order. The rest were charged with "refusal to obey".

Even if some of the shriller charges were dismissed by an eye-rolling lefty magistrate, the best-case scenario for any of them was six months in prison. Then, for the rest of their lives, they'd be shadowed by public disorder language in a background check. Their employment prospects now had a low ceiling. Their foreign visa prospects were nil.

As for the death of nineteen-year-old Altan Rahim, shot by police after seeming to reach inside a dumpster for a potential weapon, the Ministry of the Interior's investigation was "ongoing". The expectation of legal commentators was that the shooting would be deemed justified, under the broad allowances of Article 435-1 of the French National Security Code, legislation introduced in 2017 after the Bataclan theater was stormed by the Islamic State.

Article 435-1, Val said, was known on the street as the "but terrorism" law. Dumpsters rolling along at shambling pace might not typically be considered deadly – but terrorism, your honor. The chances of the kid pulling a stray bazooka from a dumpster he reached into at random might typically be considered low – but terrorism, your honor.

Those were the justifications the officer who'd fired the shots would make to a high court of silk paranoia – but terrorism, but terrorism – and they'd be accepted. Better one dead innocent than a thousand dead innocents. Security for all meant the sacrifice now and then of a kid who, it turns out, was just reaching for his iPhone. The position adopted when it wasn't *white* kids sacrificed. A reversion to pagan ideology, paid for by the Black and the brown.

Val had tried several times to write a poem for Altan, and then for the arrested protestors. She found herself blocked by a sense of guilt.

I stayed in safety, she would shrug morosely.

I might have pointed out that to be an effective voice for others you have to breathe steadily yourself. But I kept quiet. Aphorisms from the lady in furs on the sidelines. Who needs them?

On the park bench today, Val said, "Here."

She brought something out from her pocket, and motioned for me to take it. Notepaper, folded harshly around something. "I think maybe I take too many. Could you please..."

I unfolded the paper just enough to see: pills, dozens of them. Ibuprofen.

I'd suspected, of course, so what little surprise I felt I processed quickly.

I said, "You'll be alright? Cold turkey, I mean."

"I don't think it's gone that far."

"Okay." I pocketed her little package. "Done."

And it was.

There was a quiet time, the dog's leash dipping and stretching and leaving trails in the mud as it toured its anxieties.

Then Val went to her pocket again. "The show ain't over. One more thing."

She clicked it onto the bench between us.

"I went back for it," Val shrugged. "It was still right there where I left it."

I grinned. "No one stole it? Incredible."

Broken glass, about the size of a postage stamp, with a yellowish tint. She'd confronted me with this in the library.

We smiled either side of the glass on the bench, then Val put it back inside a tissue and returned it to her pocket.

She said, "You know, back at Etienne's" – the garage of the high school friend – "Writing to English pop music like that? I was lit up all over. My whole mind. It's never come out like that before, so easy and right."

"A good song will do that."

Val laughed. "That's not it." She reached to my hair and wove her fingers in. "You..." She brought the words very close to my ear. "You light me the fuck up."

She didn't move away. I didn't want her to. I sat in the certainty of that for a moment, the soft gloat of the lake water emphasizing there was no hurry.

I said, "So we do this."

"Ah, Céleste..." Her snort sent warmth down my neck and under my collar. "We've always been doing this."

I breathed then, because I hadn't yet, and Val's fingers moved to my earlobes, to work the soft hinges of my face. I accelerated things, and our mouths met. The shock of it was delicious, how immediately fierce it was, our tongues adding understrokes of tenderness and hints of espresso, cinnamon, cigarettes. I loved even that last thing. Who'd have figured.

She would come home with me after this, and we wouldn't leave my apartment for an entire day.

But first we stayed on the bench awhile, Valérie stretched out along it with her head in my lap. The dog turned to look at us, as though we could explain this terrible feeling it had. I made sympathy noises and threw some twigs for lack of a stick because I couldn't, though. I really couldn't.

"Tell me a story," Val said. "A true story."

"About?"

After more silence, she said, "Decide as you go along."

Afterword On Adama Traoré

The death of Adama Traoré on July 19th 2016 is a true event. In Beaumont-sur-Oise, a suburb of Paris in which he was also born, Adama, a Black Frenchman, fled a police ID-check. He was subsequently pinned to the ground by three officers as they arrested him. Soon afterward, Adama complained of breathing difficulties and lost consciousness. A little over an hour later, in the courtyard of a police station in nearby Persan, Adama died.

A state report proposed heart failure as the cause of death and that underlying medical conditions and cannabis use were contributing factors. An autopsy commissioned by Adama's family asserted that he died because of suffocation he experienced during his arrest.

Although Adama's family and supporters continue to agitate for justice, French magistrates closed the investigation into his death in September 2023, with no charges filed against any officer.

Real-life street art in Paris highlighting the parallels between Adama Traoré's death and the murder of George Floyd in the United States can be seen at website **redvelvetnothing.com**.

By happenstance, the day on which Adama died was also his twenty-fourth birthday.

– Z.M.B.

Trois Poèmes

Écrits à Paris

Passing (Young Rage)

Young rage smashed a window, three doors down.
You saw it when you went for bread:
A tarot store with no clear relation
To the government. Collateral damage,
Whose shattered glass snickers under the feet
Of home-comers – drunk, some of them, or
Reduced to just two senses by the assembly line.
We hear the flameless cremation of the
Window's remains as we eat. Then:
We burrow under this punishing air,
Stripping the mattress, stripping ourselves,
Waiting out the night as though the day
Will be any better. Belleville, the new tropics.
Heat waves peeling the shoulders of
The globe, and we're glad suddenly
We can't have kids. Making lab rats for
The future, in which mankind might be
A fringe interest. We'll pass.
We ask only to keep our heads. We toke
Back and forth, self-crafted fingers
Of Moroccan tobacco that point grandly
At nothing, directions from a roadside
Bum. We are never getting out of here.

Still, we juice fruit in our mouths,
And play Lakmé too loud, climbing it

To the roof of the sky. Tenderness,
There is that too. Your body diffident,
Recently vacated by a ruinous desire.
Mine restless in its exploration,
Lingering too little, delivering only
Haphazard pleasure. But what is
Coined, conjugated, vocabularized
Only now, only here, by only us,
At last breaks into fluency, and
I pin down your hands in that triumph.
Only us. The future that is bleeding heat
Into today dilates to science fiction
For a while. Sheetless, we lie rude to
The incoming breeze, dawn now curious
On the walls. The footfall down below
Has no further news of the broken window,
Or else it is powdery, too soft – lost in
The city's rising gnaw at its chains.
I know what you would say: who brings
Glass into the world without knowing
Someday it will break.

Wishes It Were A Dialogue

The third time we broke up, she'd dropped a glove
On the way over – by Gare Austerlitz, she said.
Then our argument, and her half-turned final word,
After which I soon observed my empty apartment
Was lousy to drink with, no tact about the past.
I took to the boulevard, pale and free, watching
The Pigalle hookers pause then disregard me.

I went to Gare Austerlitz. The turning circle,
The riverfront square, the side streets bluesy
And raffish… Dropped it, okay, but where?
Snow around, or rather, thin diarrhetic slush.
Garbage collection disrupted by Christmas;
Hungover travelers with crumpled reindeer stuff.
The sidewalks in all ways politesse rejected.

Still, I searched. Busboys doubting my purpose
Through their beards of cigarette smoke.
Urine hieroglyphs from dogs in the snow.
Their walkers a ways off, thumbing emojis,
Noting me odd. General awareness of me dourly
Flickering on. Such a fine coat for trolling
The gutter, round and round, head mulishly down.

See, darling? If only you could see, darling.
How brutally the hopeless does not intimidate me.

Atom In The Infinite

The heat of the evening invites
Indifference, but we choose
Otherwise, we always have.
The ease by the water, the ticket
South, must do without us.
We're in this room, entirely.

Rumors from the deeper universe.
That's what you call the wind.
The sun annotates the rolling manuscript
Of the earth, at least for the life
Of a shadow. Nothing stays.
Memories try, but the wetting of
The seawall is witnessed that way
Only once. The viewing glass on
What has passed is fogged with
Our breath when we look.
Or our sighs. More often that.

In the widespread scrabble of atoms
Toward meaning, my love has no
Distinction. There are a thousand
Like it. The salesman in the shabby coat
Gazing into the rain from the bar
Is not glorious, he is all of us
Who have ever promised. I promise.

Through the ages, weeping has
Sounded the same and as relentlessly.
Our story will do little about that.
The few will still profit from the
Mass inflation of hopes and fears.
The doubt flow of the clouds will
Never pause. We impact nothing,
These nights we combine our bodies
Against the limits of this life,
And seek some hint in our limbs
Of the other side. These nights,
It is only our own cells shaken.
So exquisitely shaken.

Your breath dotes on my shoulder
In the street-tinted dark where
We now lie. Faint shifts
In that dark – the trees outside,
Lazy in their sway. I fancy
For a moment they murmur of us.

Note on poetry

All the poems in *Valérie (or, Red Velvet Nothing)* were written by Zoe Marie Bel.

Acknowledgements

It might be my name on the cover, but this book exists in no small part because of the generosity with their time and spirit of so many others.

My mother Maggie was the first reader of *Valérie* – a very early version, no less, whose contours were still hazy. Her enthusiasm prompted me to keep working on it. Thank you, mum, my most steadfast (and athletic!) cheerleader. Many a great thing has begun with listening to you.

John Fuller and Hannah Croft, both writers themselves, found time alongside their own storyworlds to wag a thoughtful flashlight around in mine. The work began to resemble my hopes for it only when I followed their ideas for improvements. John's own novel *Loser* is one of my favorite reads of recent years. Hannah's historical opus-in-progress will surely become the same in the future.

Jaimie, Rich, Patty and Warren are collectively both my rock *and* a fount of inspiration, the geophysics of which we can all agree are hard to pull off. Then of course there's: Sio and Davey, Jamie and Rebecca, Elliot and Jo, Roberta, Betsy, Arwen, Lucy, Atticus, Ted, Daphne and Elizabeth. If some writers are able to carry on where others buckle, I suspect those who persevered had in their lives people a lot like you. Thank you, with all my love.

Enough "misadventured piteous overthows" already! My intentions in *Valérie*

A pair of star-crossed lovers take their life,
Whose misadventured piteous overthrows
Doth, with their death, bury their parents' strife.

–Romeo and Juliet, William Shakespeare

A love story about the work of social difference.

In a number of "star-crossed" love stories, the unsuitability of the two lovers is presented as a hang-up of the outside world, while true love gives zero fucks. Whatever their social differences exactly – rich/poor; Black/white; Montague/Capulet in Shakespeare's *Romeo and Juliet* – our lovers are celebrated for charging at love regardless. The outside world is prune-face disapproval; the lovers are heat-in-the-sheets awesome, reminding us all we are alive and but briefly that. So get loving, people.

Look. I dig this democratic view of love and ultimately support it. So he lives in his pick-up truck, making money from sperm donations and call-in radio contests. I agree that is no reason – none – why the trust-fund president of the lawn tennis association should not precipitously fall in love when she raps on his window and says, *You're parked on court number three, fuckwit.*

It's just that it takes nothing away from true love to acknowledge that such a relationship is going to need *work*. Insisting that social differences don't matter is not going to cut it. Mainly because it's a thumping great lie, one we let loose in literature for the glory and inspiration of it. The same way we set off fireworks on special occasions, and yet would not reach for a Catherine wheel to light the path to the tool shed. There is glorious, and then there's practical. Enjoy the show, but don't try it at home. (I mean, Shakespeare's *Romeo and Juliet* - a romance that takes place over a mere five days, with both lovers ending up idiotically dead, and one of them very underage - should probably not be regarded as a manual for *anything*. Except, perhaps, for poetry so exquisite it's like typewritten *macarons*.)

Some real talk now. In our relationships, social differences matter. After all, they could, if left unaddressed, end those relationships. Which is to say, they matter absolutely. Ignoring them turns the drama up to eleven, sure, but it's no kind of strategy for happiness. Because the reality is, we internalize our social identities. They are part of who we are, even if they are not the essence of us. So we bring them to our most intimate moments, whether we like it or not.

In those star-crossed love stories I would criticize as "no work" narratives, we don't see the lovers experience and navigate this reality in their private interactions. Juliet, soon after meeting her inconvenient beau, asks: "Wherefore art thou Romeo?" In modern English: *Why must you be Romeo, a goddamn Montague?* So far, so human. And yet this agitated thought to herself is the last time we see their conflicting social identities surface as a problem between them when alone. We never witness a moment of Romeo being vexingly *Montague* with Juliet. Or Juliet making a comment that Romeo finds just *soooo* Capulet.

Any two lovers with differences (all lovers, then) will find this weirdly bloodless and/or whimsically unrealistic. Come on... there'd be eye-rolling, ribbing ("Wow, way to Montague", "Once a Capulet, forever a...") and bickering by Act Two. Because all of us are, in some way, different. Love is not ignoring that. It's agreeing to the continual surprise of it. Sometimes surprises bother us. They just do.

In the "no work" love stories I see, all the problems of the two lovers are depicted as imposed on them by the outside world, a state of co-victimhood that brings them even closer. There is no acknowledgement that the world is not just "out there" but right here too, in their atoms, and that their relationship has the best chance of survival if they make allowances for that from day one. In these stories, our lovers ultimately either (i) succumb tragically to the world's hostility (Shakespeare/indie movie/any LGBT movie before the 2000s); or (ii) defy that hostility by peeling off in a red Corvette to some balmy but vague Other Place (any LGBT movie since the 2000s/yogurt commercial).

In *Valérie*, I wanted to show two lovers who have the self-respect (and respect for each other) to recognize that their social differences might be more than their prospective union can take – unless they do the work. That means talking about their differences, without rancor or self-defensiveness. It means, where necessary and possible, preemptively or routinely containing those differences.

It means open-minded immersion in each other's worlds (Céleste's visit to Seine-Saint-Denis, for example) and each other's worldview (Valérie's choice to adopt Céleste's mindset toward her steady job).

As I show them going about this work, I want their relationship to very much retain its chemistry. I don't think real talk or real work has to be unerotic. In fact, there might be nothing hotter than a meeting of the eyes with a recognition rush not of *We're so similar* but *We're so different...*

A love story in which love is not the problem.

The pivotal question in *Valérie* is not whether the love is there. It's whether both women can (and want to) make the changes that acting on that love would need from them (at least, if acting on it is not to be a short-lived disaster). There are plenty of scenarios I can think of in which two people might sincerely love each other but should nonetheless stay the heck away from union if they care at all about themselves, one another, or anyone else. Frankly, love in itself is not enough. A love story that acknowledges this, even if that's en route to a happy ending, feels to me more sophisticated than a story in which the central problem is the feeling itself: the love not being there yet, or there enough, or inconveniently pledged to some other guy, et cetera.

A contemporary update on what it means to be an artist in Paris.

I was an artist in Paris for three years, albeit an artist with an income steadier and higher than Valérie's. France has a far more advanced support system for artists than other countries I have experienced. Nonetheless, it can be grueling to survive as an artist in contemporary Paris. Val's solution – to draw on her 'social capital' and borrow apartments (or just about habitable spaces) rather than paying rent – may soon be the only way left for a person on a low, fluctuating income to live in Paris.

By American standards at least, Paris is a tiny city (walk it from one side to the other in some three and a half hours). It has the highest population density of any city in Europe and among the highest of cities around the world. Unlike, say, New York City in the '80s, Paris doesn't really have any conveniently empty warehouses for artist collectives to occupy (when Valérie does find such a warehouse, on Left Bank, working class and disabled folks are already living there, they too at the mercy of the insane rents of this city).

All in all, the Hemingway tropes of a writer journaling with a cigarette at a cafe by some cobblestones feel very outdated to me. In *Valérie* I want to present an updated and grimmer vision of what it means to be an artist in Paris: specifically, that even as the beauty and history of the city make artistic prowess feel so very close, it's really, really hard to make a life of it, even for the most earnest and talented of artists. I want this to be a low-key anxiety throughout the novel.

I also want to present a different vision of what is meant by **art** in Paris. For the first of my three years in Paris, the country was in pandemic lockdown, which meant one of the few things I could legally do was take long walks. I got to know the topography of the city very well, and very soon noticed its prolific and vibrant street art. While I never saw a poem embedded in a mural, I saw quoted speech and protest slogans that came very close to poetry. My imagination simply completed what those works had started. (I should note here, if it isn't obvious already: the poems "by Valérie Chaibi" are, in fact, by me.)

A huge small story.

If what happens in *Valérie* were listed down, it's not a lot.

Some library books are overdue, a picture frame falls over, two women drift through the rain to the Seine, and so on. In this story, I specifically wanted to refrain from terrorists-on-Air-Force-One level plotting and instead to focus on slight happenings that are nothing much to the world but are absolutely huge to these two women. Fixing a picture frame hardly warrants an entry on Wikipedia, and yet it is enormous when it is properly understood as an act of long-repressed love. Same with Valérie getting her job back.

There are moments in our lives that mean very little outside of our chosen universe but, within it, are our futures turning. *Valérie* is my way of remembering and honoring that.

Zoe Marie Bel, July 2024

Zoe Marie Bel

Zoe Marie Bel is a writer of fiction and poetry, whose work has appeared in *The Los Angeles Review*, *The New York Times*, *Australian Book Review*, *Mystery Tribune*, and more. Her debut short story collection *Hard Place Rock* and debut novel *After The Angels* are forthcoming. Her poetry slimbook *Foothills* is in bookstores now. Zoe lived in Paris for three years during the pandemic, and wrote *Valérie* while there.

Find out more about Zoe's work, read online pieces and follow news at **ZoeMarieBel.com**. For photography of *Valérie*'s Paris and for online features related to the novella, visit **RedVelvetNothing.com**.

www.ingramcontent.com/pod-product-compliance
Lightning Source LLC
Chambersburg PA
CBHW031330060726
47590CB00007B/2417